"Ah, you like fireworks, do you?"

Unexpected humor intensified the gleam in Richard's eyes. "Why doesn't that surprise me? You're like a firework yourself."

"A rocket?"

She was flirting with the man! What was wrong with her? They didn't even have a five-minute future together, so why encourage him?

"There are similarities, but no. One of those maddening crackers that fizz and bang and never jump the way you expect them to," he decided wickedly. "Now, those are definitely dangerous."

Challis gave him a slow, devastating smile. "So back off."

"No."

And, help her, she didn't want him to. Fatal. Richard Dovale and her—it just wouldn't do, wouldn't work for a minute. Different worlds, she reminded herself. They were diametric opposites in every way.

JAYNE BAULING was born in England and grew up in South Africa. She always wrote, but was too shy to show anyone until the publication of some poems in her teens gave her the confidence to attempt the romances she wanted to concentrate on, the first-published being written while she was attending business college. Her home is just outside Johannesburg, a town house ruled by a seal point cat called Ranee. Travel is a major passion; at home it's family, friends, music, swimming, reading and patio gardening.

Jayne Bauling

A RECKLESS SEDUCTION

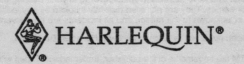

HARLEQUIN®

TORONTO • NEW YORK • LONDON
AMSTERDAM • PARIS • SYDNEY • HAMBURG
STOCKHOLM • ATHENS • TOKYO • MILAN • MADRID
PRAGUE • WARSAW • BUDAPEST • AUCKLAND

ISBN 0-373-18745-9

A RECKLESS SEDUCTION

First North American Publication 2001.

This edition published by arrangement with Harlequin Books S.A.

Visit us at www.eHarlequin.com

Printed in U.S.A.

CHAPTER ONE

CHALLIS FOX sat with her chair turned sideways to the coffee shop table on which she rested one elbow, her hand supporting her head.

She stared unseeingly at her trendy black boots. Miles was late. He had promised to be here ten minutes before the time Kel Sheridan was due to arrive.

Gradually she became aware of someone standing motionlessly beside her, someone wearing a suit, so not Miles or one of the café staff, and definitely not Sheridan. She lifted her head and let her gaze travel slowly upward, a considerable distance as he was very tall, only to discover the dark head bent, the face consequently shadowed.

He was examining her boots! And well he might, considering the rest of her outfit, the fluttery white bits and pieces of some chiffony fabric that made up her dress, the black velveteen waistcoat she wore over it and her great-grandmother's jet beads. It wasn't what she would usually have chosen for this hour of the morning—at which she was normally still in bed—and it didn't really reflect her taste at any hour of the day. It was what she thought of as her working uniform. As a DJ for Sounds FM, she had to attend a luncheon bash being thrown by the local representatives of an overseas record company after the meeting with Sheridan, and this was her own idiosyncratic adaptation of what the fashion police decreed alternatives were wearing this month, or at least this week.

As if sensing her attention, the man was raising his shapely head. Challis produced her vivacious smile, ready as always to be friendly. Her natural inclination was to take people on trust, although her semicelebrity status had taught her a degree of wariness. But she ought to be safe here, in a public place where she was known to the personnel, as she was in most of the fashionable bistros and clubs in this Rosebank area of Johannesburg.

Only, quite suddenly, she didn't feel safe! What colour were his eyes—honey, amber, topaz? It didn't matter. They were bedroom eyes and she recognised a leaping inner excitement for what it was and decided she must be losing her mind. So he had sexy eyes, and a sexy mouth, but look at that immaculate suit! She was no expert on such things, but it looked as expensive as it was beautiful; likewise the perfectly knotted tie and pristine shirt. Taste and money, but only a man, and not her kind of man at all. Still sexy, though.

He was staring at her now.

'Oh, I just got up too early.' She dismissed her misguided excitement with a scornful mutter as she straightened her chair.

'Ah,' he said. 'Is that what it was? Your eyes weren't properly open yet when you went to your wardrobe... Challis Fox? May I?'

He had moved, all grace and controlled power, and was hooking out the chair opposite hers. Startled, Challis stared at him. This couldn't be a pick-up! Men like this one didn't fancy girls like her. Men in suits like his—and she'd glimpsed that watch too—didn't pick up women or girls full-stop.

'Sorry, I'm expecting someone,' she murmured swiftly, but he still sat down.

'Kel Sheridan? He won't be meeting you.' His voice was deep and attractive, but dismissive.

She essayed another, less spontaneous smile, and that tiger's glance flicked to her vivid mouth.

'I get it! You're his dad and you do not approve!'

Sexy eyes flashed, fascinatingly.

'How old do you think I am?'

'Oh, now I've insulted you.' An extrovert, who enjoyed people too much to ever want to offend, Challis was amused but sincerely apologetic. 'Sorry, I didn't mean to. My brain just doesn't work this early in the morning... I've got no idea how old you are—obviously too young to be his old man—but you know, I have to say this whole scenario smacks of the heavy father bit, your pitching in like this and announcing Kel won't be keeping our date. All right, shall I guess again? His big brother?'

'Uncle.' A pause, seemingly deliberate, but when she continued looking expectant, he added his name, 'Richard Dovale.'

'Diamonds!' she exclaimed, in triumphant identification, and her dark blue eyes sparkled as brilliantly as the jewels she'd named.

Richard Dovale. She knew who he was. President and CEO of Dovale Diamonds. She had even seen a photo of him, a little monochrome passport-type thing, because he had refused to co-operate with the women's magazine which had recently named him one of South Africa's most eligible bachelors. She had probably seen him elsewhere too, dull head-and-shoulders shots in the business sections of newspapers, or interviews out on financial programmes on television, but she never really looked at those folk. Even the women tended to wear suits.

He was smiling—actually for the first time, she absorbed—but it was hard and cynical.

'You lack subtlety, Ms Fox. Most women dissemble madly on realising, coming across as if diamonds are the last thing on their minds and mean nothing to them.'

He was looking her over, those cat's eyes, jewel eyes, sliding insolently over her fair skin and brilliant mouth, lingering briefly on the sleekly shining cap of her black hair, alive with blue lights and curling round and in to her lively face like the petals of some strange midnight-coloured chrysanthemum, mainly because she hadn't bothered to do much with it after emerging, wincing, from the torture of her early-morning shower.

Challis laughed at him. 'What do I need to be subtle for? I mean—diamonds! Such gorgeous things! I've got a tiny little diamond earring, just a stud... Oh, the sort of thing you'd probably curl your lip at and toss to the nearest disadvantaged person you saw, the setting's so plain.'

'We're a mining company, not a jewellery outlet.' His glance noted and dismissed the two pieces of soft Thai silver adorning her left ear, and then the single fine little hoop on her right. 'You do chatter, don't you? I postponed a meeting to be here, so I can't waste time.'

It was unfriendly, an attitude she rarely encountered, and it produced in her an odd, unaccustomed inner heat, something like anger.

'So what's your problem?' she demanded insolently, giving in to the feeling, rashly confrontational
where she usually danced on the agreeable side of the
line between teasing and the aggression or insult of
overt challenge. 'How did you know about this meeting with Kel anyway?'

'This assignation?' He watched her roll her eyes at
the old-fashioned term. 'I checked his telephone messages on the way out this morning.'

'He lives with you? Like a poor relation or something? Oh, but he has his own phone number!'

'Our family arrangements are private, but I can tell
you that I've sent him and his mother off to Mauritius
for a few days.'

Challis might have had some quip to make about
that, but her favourite waiter appeared just then, having been told she was expecting someone and assuming Richard Dovale was that person—but where was
Miles? Not that she wanted or needed him. She could
handle this. She was enjoying herself, and it was only
ten o'clock in the morning! Breakfast was served until
noon here, so she ordered a large cup of coffee and
eggs Benedict. Mr Diamonds Dovale requested coffee—for form's sake, she guessed, because he was too
conventional to sit down in a coffee shop and not have
something.

She grabbed the opportunity to study him while his
attention was removed from her, and something struck
her as strange. The suit did nothing to diminish his
sheer, blatant allure. It should have. Suits usually hid,
disguised or at the very least neutralised a man's raw
reality. Not this man's, or she wouldn't be so acutely
aware of him, with this live current of half-angry excitement flickering through her veins, tempting her to

flirt, to throw out challenges, to perhaps even be friendly, if only to see what it produced from him. She suddenly remembered the magazine piece had said he was thirty-three, so no wonder he had been annoyed by her assumption that he was Kel's father! But it did make him ten years her senior, a gap that usually left her cold, so what was going on? Why this vibrant consciousness of how long and lean he was, of a leashed strength, both physical and mental, of his essential maleness? And that wasn't all she liked. There was also his nose and cheekbones, his jawline too, the warm colour of his eyes, the rich golden-brown tone of his skin, the thick, smooth darkness of hair swept back from a high, intelligent brow, and, above all, the harshly sensual curve of his mouth... Oh, sensual even when it was cynically contemptuous. She resisted looking at his hands, almost afraid of doing so, because hands were important, and if his were as perfect as the rest of him...

He caught her staring as the waiter retreated, and his attractively shaped dark eyebrows rose enquiringly in response to her furiously thoughtful frown.

Challis laughed dismissively, her brow smoothing. 'Just something that struck me as strange.'

'What struck *me* as strange was your message to Kel.' He was obviously uninterested in hearing what might be puzzling her. 'If the two of you have already got sufficiently up close and personal for him to have proved he's *good*—which surprises me in view of his youth, I might add—then it seems incongruous that you should have felt a need to tell him your surname. Although that made it easy for me to have a check run on you. But perhaps you didn't get round to exchanging such trivia as surnames in the heat of discovering how "good" he was.'

Challis stared at him in disbelief, startled by what he seemed to be implying. What had she said to Kel Sheridan? She thought back.

'*Kel? It's Challis Fox. You are good, real good. I'm impressed; I surrender. Let's do breakfast at Amakofikofi, ten tomorrow—that's Tuesday—unless I hear from you before then...*'

It had gone something like that anyway. She had definitely used 'I' rather than 'we', although Miles Logan had been equally impressed by the DJ's equivalent of a demo-tape which the young man had submitted to Sounds FM. But she had been the first to listen to it after Security had screened the package, because it had been addressed to her, delivered by courier and packaged to intrigue, done up in a flurry of pastel satin ribbons with a little net frill of sugared almonds attached, suggesting some grasp of the value of hype, although that hadn't been what had prompted her to take the tape to Miles.

Richard Dovale was watching her intently, a pronounced gleam of derisive challenge in the golden-brown eyes, and small wonder, if he thought she had seduced his nephew.

'I can just imagine the sort of check someone like you can command,' she mocked, to give herself time to decide how she was going to deal with this. 'What do they call you, a magnate? Tycoon? Mogul? Why haven't you sent some minion along instead of getting your own hands dirty? Oh, but I suppose you preferred to take care of it yourself. That way there's less likelihood of this—this aberration on the part of a family member becoming public knowledge. Is this where you offer to pay me off? Or do I mean buy me?'

'How much?' The prompt response was made in a hard voice, matched by his expression, with not even a tremor of a smile to suggest that he knew she was teasing him.

'Not even a bagful of your brightest, shiniest diamonds,' she snapped, upset at being so misunderstood.

'You think you'll do better in the long term by continuing to be a threat to Kel?' Richard Dovale suggested, more contemptuously than anyone had ever spoken to her before.

'No, because in the first place I'm not a threat to your nephew,' she began, deciding that this was the generation gap yawning between them and that it was time to tell him she had been joking.

'He's only eighteen,' he inserted tautly.

'I was about to mention it,' she agreed drily.

'So?' Blankly. 'How old are you?'

'Twenty-two.'

'The last woman he got mixed up with was twenty-six,' he told her flatly.

'More fool her, then.'

'No, Kel was the fool, because she damn nearly had him trapped.' A pause, the sexy mouth curving disparagingly. 'It's not that he's in any way naïve, but he's heavily into self-gratification and seldom looks ahead in the heat of the moment.'

'And?' Challis prompted innocently. 'Because I don't think you're doing this—warning me of his flawed character—to protect me from what sounds like a normal young man's natural selfishness... are you?'

There was a slight pause as he studied her, seemingly looking for something specific. Once again, with silence between them, Challis felt her awareness of him surging, a hot exhilaration. It wasn't just the way he looked, admittedly magnificent, if too conventional for her taste. There was something else—a vibe, she identified at last, a sensual energy that emanated from him.

He smiled very slightly. 'I doubt if you're in any need of protection, although... You know, you're quite incredible to look at.'

She sighed theatrically, although she was startled.

'My clothes again?' she guessed resignedly.

'No, it's you. You look so bright and self-reliant, full of confidence, but then there's that fair skin of yours, the most delicate-looking I've ever seen.'

That surprised her even more. It was so open, a frank comment of the kind she would never have expected from such a man, and not even the sort of remark she was used to receiving from those men who *did* comment on her looks.

'It sounds as if you don't like contradictions,' she observed impulsively.

'I don't.'

'Because they make you have to think?'

'Because they arouse my suspicion.' He paused as the waiter arrived with their coffee, murmuring that Challis's eggs would follow shortly. 'But this is wasting my time—and you're wasting yours chasing my nephew, whatever your motives, material or otherwise. And if they're not material you surprise me. What can you see in a boy like that?'

'We're back to the age-gap?' Challis just couldn't resist teasing him a little longer, mainly because she had never met anyone like him before, and anticipating his reactions was an adventure. 'That's so conventional. Why does the male have to be the older partner in a relationship? Haven't you ever been involved with an older woman? You should try it. It's well known that we mature emotionally much earlier than men do, but on the other hand our libido reaches its full strength quite late, at a time when it's all downhill for a man of the same age.'

She was lightly mischievous, hoping to make him laugh, or at least smile properly, prompted by some obscure urge to see him relaxed and amused.

'Then you've got a long way to go, haven't you?' It was humour of a kind, but not her kind, utterly deadpan. 'Twenty-two isn't mature.'

'Just too mature for eighteen? Actually, I already have a boyfriend,' she added gently, needing to make herself clear.

'Yes, you would have. But with you coming from the world you do, I have to wonder if he's a permanent fixture?'

'I don't know yet.' It was the simple truth, for if her relationship with Serle was progressing at all, then it seemed to be doing so in the wrong direction.

'I also wonder whether you confine yourself to one boyfriend at a time, and how literally you mean the "boy" bit?' Richard went on.

'I'd probably still call him a boyfriend if he was *your* age. He's not, but he's not as young as Kel either. Thanks.' She smiled at the waiter as he placed her order in front of her, following it with a sudden uncontrollable yawn, raising a slim hand to cover her mouth, slender fingers tipped with gleaming oval nails flawlessly painted with translucent white. 'Sorry. I work nights.'

'I know.'

'How? You don't fit our listener profile—oh! That check you ran,' she realised belatedly, laughing. 'For a tiny moment there I thought you might be offering me a spectacularly antiquated insult.'

'No, I assure you I wasn't.' Ultra-cool, pausing calmly to take a mouthful of coffee. 'For all I know you're a model of integrity in your professional life, with any acquisitiveness reserved for private enterprises—Kel being your current focus. How much did he tell you about his family? Not too much, obviously, as you didn't know who I was, but enough for you to have sussed that there's money. At best, as you're clearly clever, you're probably an opportunist, so I'm sure you'll understand that I'm ready to act to prevent the damage someone like you could inflict on my family.'

'Damage!' Indignation lifted her voice. 'Let me tell you, your precious nephew made the approach, here, and it wasn't the first one either. I've never actually met him, but Security say he's been known to hang around the foyer at Sounds FM. I have seen him from a distance, though, when he's appeared at the club gigs I have to DJ under my contract with the station—Why are you looking like that? Have I offended you again? No member of your élite family could possibly be chasing someone like me! Believe it. He tries to contact me on the Internet, or calls me when I open the lines on my show; he faxes me and leaves voice-mail at other times. Oh, he's a legitimate fan, and he's always been upfront about his identity, if not about his connections. You were right about that.'

'It sounds as if you have considerable experience of another type of fan.'

He spoke with the same distaste that had transformed his expression when she had told him about his nephew's behaviour. Challis lifted a shoulder, her bright mouth curving ruefully.

'Stalkers. It goes with the territory.'

'The image.' It was a sardonic correction.

'Whatever. Look, Richard—oh, is that all right, or do I have to call you Mr Dovale? Or maybe even sir, considering the social gulf?' she digressed, gently taunting because he was taking everything, including her, far too seriously, and it was time he understood that she didn't pose any threat to Kel. 'Richard, my interest in Kel is strictly professional.'

'If what you've said about him being such a besotted fan is true, then it's not exactly "professional" of you to be encouraging him.' The sceptical tone made it clear that he was reserving judgement.

'Except that part of his interest in me is professional. Anyway, there are a hundred different ways of looking at the situation, all sorts of grey areas,' she argued tartly, incensed by the criticism. 'Who's to say what's right or wrong?'

'Knowing right from wrong exercises your mind?' Eyes that ought to be warm, if only because of their rich firelight colour, were cool and contemptuous.

'I don't suppose you ever have any trouble there?' Challis prompted waspishly, losing her head slightly because his constant disparagement was beginning to make her angry. 'I might have known a man like you would be a black-and-white moralist. I bet you have rules for everything in your life, don't you?'

He didn't respond at once, seemingly intrigued by

the changes anger wrought in her face as he studied her, his glance encompassing the sparking, dark blue fury of her eyes and the lyrically generous curve and line of her gleamingly coloured lips.

'Some of which I'm occasionally tempted to break,' he finally conceded drily, but gave her no chance to take him up on that, demanding abruptly, 'So tell me why you're really interested in my nephew?'

'Because he's phenomenally talented!' Challis never stayed angry for long, and she rushed into the overdue explanation eagerly, now that he was actually condescending to give her the opportunity. 'He sent me a tape of himself in DJ mode and it's fantastic. I got our station manager and programme director— same guy in our case—to listen to it, and he agrees. We want him.'

'No way.' Just the two words, utterly implacable.

'Why not? I don't know how much you know about us: we're a little independent consortium-owned music station, with a listenership aged mainly between the early teens and mid-twenties—thirty tops.' She continued to make her pitch, ignoring his impatient expression. 'The airwaves are crowded since deregulation, and the competition is stiff, but we're the best and we're staying the best. If we don't grab Kel Sheridan, one of our rivals will.'

'He's not doing radio work.'

'Who says?' she demanded, beginning to find his flat, brief rejections frustrating. 'He's eighteen, old enough to vote and drive a car—old enough to choose his own career. Look, we wouldn't give him his own show immediately, he'd have to do at least six months on the technical side, producing, with just the occa-

sional stand-in or graveyard shift—one to four a.m.—
to give him experience. That's our policy.'

'You're wasting your time and mine,' Richard
stated tautly, unmoved by her switch to sweet reason,
ignoring the sincere appeal with which she was regarding him.

'What about Kel's? This could be a stepping stone
to a more serious career for him, so why be so disparaging about it?' She felt a surge of anger when this
failed to alter his expression. 'Oh, maybe Kel doesn't
need to work, and maybe you've forgotten— No,
wait, Dovale Diamonds have existed for ever! So
maybe you simply can't relate to those of us who still
have to make a living. Jobs aren't sitting up and beg-
ging, you know, and people of my age are usually
told we're too inexperienced for those that are. Music
radio offers us a chance, a start—valuable training for
the future. Kel won't always be young. He'll go on
to other media work, and this will have given him a
good grounding.'

'Other *entertainment* work.'

'I do what I have to do for now, but I don't look
on it as the entertainment business. We're part of the
media.' Seeing his look, she went on swiftly, 'Yes, I
know that covers a lot, but we're on the respectable,
responsible side.'

It had no effect. 'Just don't contact my nephew
again, Ms Fox.'

She looked at him, declining to make any promises.

'I suppose you erased my message?' she guessed
distractedly.

'What do you think?' he retorted grimly.

Her lovely, usually vivacious face hardened.

'Think? I think you're a control freak. I know your type.'

'Anathema to someone like you,' he agreed, and smiled cynically. 'You see, I know yours.'

'So what are you doing here, sitting at this table with a whole bunch of people staring and probably recognising both of us?' she countered rather wildly, because his inflexible attitude was upsetting her, although she wasn't sure why. 'I'm surprised you were willing to risk it.'

'Why?' Unexpectedly, he seemed genuinely curious.

Challis smiled mockingly. 'Well, you see, in my own way I'm a celebrity, at least in this city.'

'A minor one, but I'll concede the point. You even have stalkers!' he agreed, caustically theatrical. 'But go on.'

'So how can you risk being seen with me, the possibility that we may be identified?' she challenged. 'Wouldn't it cause you terrible embarrassment?'

'Because you're so young and funky?' he guessed.

'And you're so old and conventional,' she supplemented, in no mood to consider any sensitivity he might possess, especially as she didn't think he did. 'Actually, it's just occurred to me that it works both ways. I could lose all my credibility if I'm seen fraternising with someone so conventional.'

'So if ever you and I decided to have an affair, it would have to be a secret one, wouldn't it?' he submitted smoothly, a gleam of real humour in the golden eyes.

Challis was completely unprepared. His candid reference to such a possibility was the last thing she would have expected from a man of his kind and age, especially when they had only just met and the meeting hadn't been exactly agreeable. She searched his hard, dark face. She had found his maleness distracting from the start, but it simply hadn't entered her mind that he might be viewing her as anything other than a threat to his nephew.

'Am I supposed to take that seriously?' she demanded on a gasp of disbelieving laughter. 'No, of course I'm not. We come from such different worlds.'

'True, and just as well, probably,' he agreed easily, still slightly amused, but then he added seriously, 'Will you leave my nephew alone, Challis?' As if he had finally sussed that the way to get to her was with that sort of open, undisguised appeal.

Challis stared back at him, seeing something reluctant darkening his eyes and pulling his mouth into a harshly brooding shape.

'You hate being here, doing this, don't you?' She voiced a sudden lightning shaft of insight.

Richard looked at her in silence for several seconds, as if surprised or disconcerted that she should have gauged that.

'Yes,' he finally confirmed heavily.

It happened all too often, empathy leading to compassion and thus weakening her position whenever she detected real unhappiness.

'And will it make for strained family relationships if we do go after Kel?' she probed gently.

'And worse,' he acknowledged tersely. 'But the details are private. If it helps, I'm not doing this for Kel. Someone else.'

Kel's mother, she guessed. Richard's sister, since the surnames were different, she worked out.

'OK, I'll think about what you've said,' she allowed easily.

He scrutinised her relaxed expression sceptically. 'Why this sudden capitulation?'

'You're not a very trusting person, are you?' She acknowledged his natural suspicion.

'I've never found much reason to be.'

She sighed and shrugged. 'It's not exactly capitulation, just a promise to think about what you've said.'

'Why?'

'Because—oh, I don't know.' Her gesture expressed frustration over her inability to articulate it. 'Because an unhappy family... That's bad.'

'And I'm to be satisfied with that? I suppose I'll have to be.' He looked at his watch, produced a wallet and extracted a note, which he placed on the table, before pushing back his chair impatiently. 'For your breakfast. I can't hang around.'

He stood up, and on impulse she too rose to her feet, holding out a hand as she gave in to a small temptation.

'Shall we shake hands?' she invited him.

He glanced down at her outstretched hand and laughed, a warmly attractive sound that somehow touched her physically, making her skin tingle.

'I wouldn't have thought you'd attach any importance to such a convention.'

'Oh, I do,' Challis insisted happily. 'A lot of importance. Touching lets you learn something about the other person. Not everything, naturally, but it provides a fundamental clue or two.'

And she was never going to get to touch him in an any more intimate way. As they had agreed, they came from different worlds.

Which might be a pity but was also probably just as well, she concluded as a strong brown hand closed firmly round her fair one, its attractive shape and size as fatally alluring as she had feared. His touch did things for her too, as she had known it would, sending warm, powerful sensations shooting through her.

Perhaps the physical contact was doing something similar to him. Now that she was standing up, he was subjecting her figure to a raking scrutiny, with particular reference to her proud, full breasts—for the first time, she realised, and that was unusual. Most men couldn't stop staring at her breasts, some even commented, whereas the only aspect of her appearance to have drawn comment from Richard was her skin! Not that she had ever really minded. That was the way men were and she was feminine enough to be proud of her figure. They were nice high breasts, spectacular in conjunction with her ultra-slim body.

Richard Dovale's attention didn't exactly bother her. It *excited* her, and after a mindless moment she decided that this morning's meeting had been quite enough. Attraction took no account of personalities, and she and this man would drive each other mad in a day, so different were they in every way.

'Keep your promise,' he reminded her on a steely note, and released her hand.

Challis sank back on to her chair and watched him leaving the coffee shop, just as her boss Miles Logan walked in, dressed in his customary baggy jeans and a Madiba shirt. Miles took a look as they passed each other. Richard didn't, staring straight ahead, his dark head at a confident angle.

Typical, Challis thought.

'I just saw Richard Dovale.' Miles threw himself

on to the chair Richard had vacated. 'Sorry I'm so late, sugar, and I couldn't call. I just had my phone taken off me—at the same traffic light I had my shades ripped off my face last month, can you believe?—so I detoured to have a nervous breakdown at the cop-shop.'

'If you will drive with the top down.'

'Who put sugar in this?' He had swallowed a mouthful of the coffee Richard had left untouched. 'Did Sheridan show up?'

'No, but his uncle did. Richard Dovale, Miles.' Their eyes met in perfect understanding. 'If we hire him, he'll have to keep it quiet or our credibility goes. To be fair, he must know the connection wouldn't fit in with our image, as he's never mentioned it, but I'm not so sure we should go with him after all. It'll cause trouble in his family, if nowhere else.'

'OK, if that's your reading,' he accepted. 'It was always going to be your baby, baby.'

'Don't call me baby, baby.'

A pleasant-faced man in his late twenties, with fashionably cut mouse-brown hair and grey eyes, Miles grinned at her, and Challis smiled back. She liked her job, and she was going to like it even more when she was the boss.

CHAPTER TWO

'ISN'T there some proper word?' Challis asked Serle Orchard delightedly. 'You know, for when you hear a word or a name or an idea for the first time and then you keep on coming across it? I met Richard Dovale the other morning and now there he is again! I wonder what he's doing here? Not pursuing me, that's for sure. The woman he's with is vaguely familiar.'

It was Saturday night, and, free of club gigs this weekend, Challis had accepted an invitation to the thrash a local music production company was holding in this plush Johannesburg convention centre to introduce their next big thing to the industry. Serle hadn't been invited—he worked for a rival label—so he had been happy to partner her. He was viewing it as an opportunity for networking and checking out the opposition.

Richard was wearing another suit. His partner was a classic beauty, in classic black—just the sort of woman Challis would have expected him to have in his life, she decided. She was tall and willowy, with sleek hair of that dark blonde shade which was nearly always natural—probably because she felt it would be beneath her dignity to lighten it.

Challis caught herself up, wondering why her thoughts were following such a bitchy line when she usually admired the sort of women whose confidence—arrogance sometimes—enabled them to demand that the world accept them as nature had produced them.

'She's Julia Keverne,' Serle told her as he located the couple. 'You know, the gold-mining family. She's the daughter—heiress, I should say.'

'Diamonds and gold, how appropriate,' Challis laughed. 'Or maybe it's one of those couplings where they'd both go partnerless if they didn't have each other. You know, too élite to associate with anyone else.'

'Could be. I've got an idea it's been going for years, but only off and on.' Serle always knew a lot about Johannesburg society. 'Her family have pumped a lot of money into backing the sort of indigenous music this label produces, so that'll be why they're here.'

'Some form of philanthropy being incumbent on such people, *noblesse oblige* and all that,' Challis observed sympathetically.

Serle wasn't evincing any similar sympathy, his slightly protuberant pale blue eyes discontented as they rested on the elegant pair who were talking to a renowned poet. Challis sighed. She had been going out with him for two months, and she was beginning to realise what a grudging nature he had, resentful of other people's happiness, success and, above all, their wealth. He had been so lavish in his flattery of her when they had first met, and he was very handsome, tall and an individualistic dresser, but was that all that had attracted her? If vanity and the fact that she was a sucker for the sort of fair, floppy hair that fell over a man's brow had done it, then it was time for a rethink.

He didn't even strike her as that attractive any

more. Challis looked for Richard Dovale again. Now *he* was more than merely attractive. Even from this distance his impact was shattering, tightening her stomach as she absorbed the physical sensuality, the beautiful colouring, the sheer sophistication—so why couldn't he have been a congenial soul from her own world?

Not that she needed a man in her life, but it was always nice to have a partner, and Serle was beginning to be a real disappointment to her.

But Mr Diamonds Dovale would be an even bigger mistake than Serle. Upright. Uptight. Responsible. Responsible for the nation's wealth, among other things—and to an impressive degree in a largely mineral-based economy, as Dovale Diamonds provided employment for a massive section of the population. Responsible for his family too, she supposed reluctantly, although she didn't like the way he had interfered in his nephew's concerns.

Seeing him separated from his partner, and with Serle now talking shop with an acquaintance, she yielded to an impulse to stroll over to Richard and say hello.

'It's truly decadent, isn't it?' she observed, finding him inspecting the lavish buffet, a banquet of delicacies presided over by awesome ice-sculptures. 'Although I have to say your expression suggests it doesn't quite measure up to your standards. I wonder if they're providing doggy-bags? I won't need to do any grocery shopping for a week!'

'I'm sure you're capable of persuading them that they are,' he returned enigmatically. 'Are you working?'

His gaze roamed slowly over her and she felt it like

a kind of sliding heat. Such warm eyes—no, hot eyes tonight—registering everything. Her special evening make-up, lips subtly sheened to echo the colour on her nails, and her satin-sleek blue-black hair, tumbling over her brow but worn back from the sides of her face to reveal her pretty ears and their accoutrements; two modest studs plus a single, beautifully carved little red rose. Nothing escaped him.

'It's one of the things I do,' Challis answered him swiftly, wondering if it had been reckless to approach him, considering what his comprehensive inspection was doing to her, 'attending these razzles.'

'You know, I can understand why you attract those stalkers you mentioned,' he observed, after another look at the filmy jacket she wore unfastened over a plain round-necked top in the same muted dark red shade, with a neat little black skirt and barely black stockings below. 'Looking the way you do.'

Her dark blue eyes blazed in response to the implied criticism.

'Am I supposed to blame myself just because some sad people haven't got a life?'

He smiled then, a slow smile, derisive, insolent and yet sensually caressing at the same time.

'Oh, it's not just the sad saps, Challis. Any man still half alive would be tempted, confronted by such a vision.'

It was proffered in a voice to match his smile, and what was this fluttering sensation, not only deep in her sex, but affecting her pulses and even her heart?

'You, for instance?' she suggested audaciously.

'If I let myself forget what I know,' he acknowledged sardonically.

Once again his candour surprised her, even if what

he knew remained obscure to her. She would never have imagined his actually admitting to—well, to being attracted to someone like her!

'Anyway, you already have someone with you,' she reminded him meltingly.

'As do you.'

'So we can't elope,' she mourned flippantly.

'You actually pay lip-service to such proprieties?'

'I imagined you did.'

He didn't confirm or deny it, digressing smoothly, 'Incidentally, this man you're with?'

'Serle Orchard.'

'Yes. Julia—that's Julia Keverne—was telling me who he is.'

'That's a coincidence,' Challis inserted blithely. 'Serle was just telling me who *she* is. I'd only seen photos before. Is she your girlfriend?'

'She invited me to accompany her tonight as her family take an interest in some of the artists on this company's list.'

It was slightly repressive, but Challis had to admire his cool.

'You're not giving anything away, are you? Do you think I'll run to the Press and sell the story if you admit anything?'

'Would you?' he enquired, as if half-expecting her to confirm it. 'My private life is just that, and as you aren't even a casual friend...'

The rest was left implied. It was fair enough, yet she felt it as a rejection, unexpectedly wounding. The feeling, the awareness of a hitherto unsuspected vulnerability incensed her. She produced a blistering smile.

'How can you deprive the headline-writers of such

a gift?' She knew she was probably asking for trouble, but she couldn't stop herself. "'Jewels for Jools!'"

He stirred exasperatedly, the smallest of movements but it made her suddenly nervous. 'I just know you're going to call me *Rich* any moment now, aren't you?'

'Well, you are,' she pointed out kindly. 'I think that's at least half your trouble. All those diamonds... That reminds me, it's all gold-mining around here, so why do you live in Johannesburg? You do, don't you?'

'It makes sense to have our head office in the nation's commercial capital, wouldn't you say?' Typically, his sense of humour emerged just when she least expected it. 'You weren't thinking I mine them personally?'

'Why not?' she shot back. 'A gold-digger like me has to do all her own work.'

'Gold-digger?' Richard considered it. 'What an antique word.'

'Just jumping up and down right there in the front of your antique mind, every time you set eyes on me,' she guessed rashly.

'With reason, it seems, if you keep insisting on it,' he snapped, visibly angry now. 'You're impossible. You've got far too much to say for yourself, so it's pointless trying to talk to you. Anyway, you probably already know and don't mind what Julia has told me about your boyfriend: that his company generally and he specifically have got somewhat grubby reputations where business practices are concerned. A tip I was insane enough to think I might owe you in return for your decision to leave Kel alone, but perhaps you find Orchard's lack of ethics appealing, because you're two of a kind, and I'd be a fool to put any faith in the promise you gave me the other day, especially when it was so nebulous.'

Infuriated by his readiness to think the worst of her, Challis spun away from him and spoke over her shoulder, tossing the words at him like missiles.

'Thank God you're no relation of mine. I pity poor Kel. Well, you may believe you have the right to interfere in his life just because he is family, but you have no right to interfere in mine. I'll judge Serle for myself, thank you very much.'

She stalked away without looking at him again, brushing past Julia Keverne in the crowd as she did so and noticing distractedly that she had beautiful, cool blue-grey eyes.

'Hey!' Serle was reproachful as she rejoined him. 'I was just going to come over and get you to introduce me to Dovale. A contact like that could be well worthwhile.'

His words decided her. And this had nothing to do with Richard's warning, she promised herself.

'I'm not sure what "worthwhile" means in your scheme of things, Serle,' she began honestly. 'Does it mean the same to you as it does to me? I think it requires some discussion.'

'Great! I was beginning to think we'd never get to the nitty-gritty. I've dropped enough hints but you've given me so few clues in return. What would be worth your while, Challis?' he urged crudely, looking gratified. 'You know how much we've got riding on our boy's new CD when we release it next week.'

Challis looked at him, accepting that it was over and should never have been begun. She laughed.

'Oh, yes, what's-his-face with the acoustic guitar.

Sorry, there's no place for him on our play-list. We gave the first song off his debut album a couple of plays and the listeners rejected it.'

'I'm not talking about daytime radio. I know all about the damned play-list.' Serle dismissed it contemptuously. 'But you play what you like on your night-time slot, so do your weekend DJs.'

'I play alternative music,' she stated proudly, 'and at weekends they're idealistic hard rockers or older hippy-types. Your guy's stuff just doesn't fit—'

'So what do you want?' he interrupted insistently.

'Haven't you got the message yet?' she demanded scornfully. 'I've been doing my best to pretend I didn't notice your attempt to bribe me—your grossly unsubtle attempt—so perhaps *I* was too subtle for you. To put it simply, then, Serle, don't say another word and never come near me again. Do you want your company blacklisted?'

Serle flushed with anger, although his expression was disbelieving. 'And what about us?'

'There is no us.' She started to turn away.

He had enough sense of self-preservation not to restrain her physically, but he followed her a couple of steps, sneering, 'Miss Morality! And I thought you were ambitious. You'll never get anywhere, never succeed, you know. You haven't got a clue about how things really work in this business.'

Challis wasn't going to dignify his words by responding. She just kept on walking, a couple of ugly epithets the last she heard from Serle before he gave up, probably for fear of attracting attention.

Typically, she only remained angry—with herself as much as with him—for a minute or two before dismissing the episode. The lesson was learnt, Miles

Logan would be informed, and any further action would be up to him.

Buoyant with a feeling of freedom, ignoring both Richard and Serle now, she worked the room with sparkling eyes and a brilliant smile, drank champagne, indulged herself at the buffet, and listened to the feature band's set before deciding it would be wise to get herself home for the treat of a comparatively early night.

The convention centre had its own beautiful grounds, and she moved towards one of several open doors, removing her cellphone from her bag.

'What are you doing?' Richard was suddenly beside her and her heart jumped—although she had been aware of his looking her way once or twice, merely kidding herself that she was ignoring him.

'Looking for some peace and quiet so I can phone for a taxi home,' she offered abruptly, sparing him only the briefest of glances as she paused in the doorway, noting the summer lightning playing across the city sky.

'Isn't the boyfriend fit to drive you?'

'We've just split up,' she admitted shortly, then caught a glimpse of his expression and added defiantly, 'but not because of anything you said earlier, so you can just stop looking like that. I've done enough of your bidding by backing off where your precious nephew is concerned. Serle is a louse. I was beginning to suspect it before you started on me. He confirmed it.'

'And you didn't waste any time dumping him,' he absorbed appreciatively, and smiled. 'We'll drive you home.'

'You and Jools?'

He laughed, the sound doing something delicious to her skin again. It was a pity his sense of humour manifested itself so rarely—or perhaps it was just that she failed to amuse him.

'I think she might find "Jools" just a little lacking in dignity. Are you ready to leave now?'

Challis contemplated the offer for perhaps five seconds, and gave in to sheer curiosity. Because this man fascinated her, was so different from her and everyone else she knew. Her curiosity was extended to his girl-friend, fiancée, lover—whatever Julia Keverne might be. She was dying to know what kind of woman appealed to a man with his knockout brand of male sensuality, what sort of woman could transform the lambent warmth of his eyes to blazing heat.

'Just as soon as I've found the waiter who was organising my doggy-bag,' she said swiftly, ruthlessly suppressing her imagination.

'Where do you live?' he asked her, when she had it and he had introduced her and Julia.

'Rosebank. Near that coffee shop,' she added.

'Then you'd better drop me off first, Richard,' Julia suggested easily.

'Makes sense,' he agreed.

They couldn't be spending the night together, then, Challis realised, a little ashamed of her speculation. Unless he meant to return to Julia after taking her home.

His car was just what she would have expected, solid, conservative and ultra-luxurious.

'So you work for Sounds FM, do you, Challis?' Julia prompted from the front passenger seat after they had joined the Saturday night traffic. 'I believe the station plays some of the artists my parents and I are sponsoring? I'm afraid I don't listen. I imagine Sounds must be very much Kel's style, Richard?'

'Too much so, if all I've been told is true,' he asserted sardonically, and Challis aimed a grimace at the back of his head.

'It must be quite amusing, being involved with a youth-orientated outfit like that,' Julia continued smoothly. 'Lots of fun, I'm sure. What do you plan to do later on?'

Challis found her difficult to read. She thought Julia was probably one of those people in whom courtesy was ingrained, hence her determination to include her, the outsider, in the conversation, and she respected that. Some women would simply have ignored her. But Julia sounded so mature, yet Challis didn't think she could be in her thirties yet.

'After I've finished fooling around, do you mean?' She couldn't resist it, aware that Richard would find it provocative, however Julia took it. 'I'd like to take over Miles Logan's job and run the station eventually.'

'That's very ambitious of you.' Julia really did sound like a nice, elderly lady humouring a child. 'Here we are.'

Like some rich adult character in a soap opera, she still lived in the family home, it seemed—the famous Keverne estate, very close to the convention centre. The place was bristling with security. One of the uniformed men shone his torch on Challis's face, and although she liked dogs, she didn't think she'd want to get close to the animal at the other end of the leash he held.

'I'll only be a minute,' Richard told her, after he and Julia had got out of the car outside what could only be called a mansion. 'Move to the front mean-while.'

She would give them five minutes to say goodnight, she decided as she complied, and then she was ringing for a taxi. And let the security guards make what they would of that. Uncharacteristically, she felt out of place, vaguely uncomfortable. Being left in the car like this let her know just how alien Richard and Julia found her.

It couldn't have been a very passionate goodnight. Richard was back in less than the stated minute.

'That woman needs some fun in her life,' she ventured spontaneously as he fastened his seat-belt.

He met her quip with silence, switching on the car's interior light and studying her compassionate expression.

'You're serious, aren't you?' he realised, and turned it off again, surprising her by adding, 'Yes, you're right. She does.'

'And you can't supply it because you do too,' she decided as he started the car.

'Fun isn't always—possible,' he stated enigmatically.

'Because being who you are is a serious business? It's a burden, isn't it, the responsibility of being so rich? And Jools is the Keverne heiress, Serle says.'

Once again it took a while for him to respond, and she hated the hard distrust she heard in his voice when he eventually did so.

'You've got us properly filed and labelled in case of opportunity, have you? Or do you make your own opportunities, Challis? Is that why you're being so sweetly understanding? Because you hope to relieve one or both of us of some or all of our financial burdens.'

'And your suspicion of everyone, which your wealth obviously engenders, is the worst burden of all,' Challis flared, angry and upset, deciding she never wanted to be seriously rich if this was what it did to you. 'When and how have I ever given you cause to think such things of me, may I ask? Or do you just always automatically assume the worst of everyone?'

'There's the way you went after Kel for one thing,' he submitted coolly.

'I explained that to you. Didn't you believe me? No, of course not, you don't believe anyone!' She was almost breathless, red rage running in her veins. 'I backed off from Kel anyway.'

'Yes, you did,' he concurred thoughtfully as the last security guard waved them off the Keverne property, and then to her absolute astonishment he said simply, 'I'm sorry. It's just difficult for me to take anyone on trust. You're very flippant a lot of the time, and I think I probably take it too seriously—or take the joke as a version of the truth anyway.'

It went straight to her heart. Challis could have cried. He was so determined not to be vulnerable, hence his suspicion of everyone, and yet he was ready to expose himself with such an explanation. That was brave.

'You keep surprising me by being so open about yourself,' she admitted, noticing that the storm was closing in, the sky full of wild electricity. 'Maybe I should try to be too, only I've never really given much thought to...well, to what I'm all about. Maybe I can start by saying I don't mean any harm to anyone.'

'It's a good start.' Pausing, he laughed deprecatingly. 'No, wait. I have to ask. What about this Miles Logan? You implied that you were acting with his approval when you tried to meet Kel, but does the man know you're after his job?'

'Fully! He wants me to have it,' she supplied promptly, all pretence abandoned. 'Stations like ours have a rapid turnover rate. We get too old too quickly. It's a stepping stone to other things for many of our personnel. Miles aims to move on, hopefully to manage a television channel. I'm his chosen successor, and the consortium who own us have hinted to him that they'll have no problem with that, although they'll probably have to advertise the position to make it legitimate. So, quite apart from the fact that your nephew was targeting me, courting me, marketing himself to me—whatever it was—he would have been my baby by the time we were ready to give him a regular slot.'

'And is that your ultimate ambition, to run the station?'

'I'm not sure. I'll probably also move on to something else later on, or start accepting more voice-overs than I'm doing now—if I'm not too busy having real babies by then.' She laughed at herself. 'And even if I am, I'm sure I could cope with both—babies and some nice job.'

'I'm sure you could,' Richard echoed her, drily meaningful.

'The only problem is, being in charge of Sounds could turn out to be dangerously seductive; you know, being a big fish in a small pond?'

'Dulling to ambition?' he suggested understandingly.

'Yes. On the other hand, I know my limitations.'

He laughed at that. 'I didn't think you'd recognise that you had any.'

'I don't know. I try to be realistic. I think I might have what it takes to do well in talk radio later on, when I've got more experience.'

'Oh, you can talk all right, but perhaps you'd be too opinionated.' Audible amusement again.

'You think I'm incapable of objectivity?' she demanded, ready to argue it out.

'Objectivity is something we acquire along with maturity, it has always seemed to me.'

'Are you sure you're old enough to know?' she teased.

'I thought you had me down as verging on ancient?' he retorted.

'Yes, well, I may have implied something of the kind, but now I'm being *objective*. You're not really that old. So you see, objectivity isn't exclusive to age.'

'I don't know,' Richard disagreed. 'For instance, some years ago I'd have viewed *you* very subjectively, and gone with that instead of trying to assess what you're really all about.'

'But now you're older you're viewing me totally objectively?' Challis wasn't really sure what he meant, but the idea still gave her an odd, almost excited feeling.

There was a pause before he said honestly, 'Trying to.'

'And failing?' she suggested, because he hadn't really accepted that she was as harmless as she claimed to be.

'We were talking about your future career options,'

he reminded her, abruptly changing the direction of the conversation.

She thought about that for a moment, before laughing dismissively. 'Of which there are several, but it's not a serious dilemma for now.'

'You don't take anything very seriously, do you? Nothing worries you.'

'I'm too busy to let it. Unless it's truly unavoidable, if something looks like troubling me I'll deny it space in my life.' She made it a bald statement in response to his note of complicated criticism.

'Too busy being young, having fun?'

'Why not? It's my life and I like it. Would you like something from my doggy-bag? A profiterole, or a meringue, or one of those mini-quiches?'

'No, thanks.'

The street they were in was well-lit, so she caught the amused glance he shot her. It didn't trouble her. She felt more relaxed with him now that he had given her a brief glimpse of the human being inside the cynical, suited exterior, and she was actually enjoying herself—most of the time.

She just wished she could give him some of the fun that was so starkly missing from his rich, responsible life, but he was ten years older than her, so their ideas of fun probably wouldn't coincide anyway.

She directed him to her flat and he found a space in the visitors' parking.

'I'll see you in,' he said as thunder rumbled overhead. 'It's about to rain.'

'Just to the lift will be fine.' Challis sent him a mischievous smile as they entered the building's well-lit foyer. 'Unless you want to come up and share my bag of goodies?'

Richard smiled very slightly, but something complex glowed in his eyes, as if disapproval warred with amusement.

'I'll pass, thanks.' He declined the invitation lightly. 'But I will see you to your door.'

Blue-white lightning flashed, thunder clapped simultaneously, and Challis squeaked as everything plunged into darkness, following it with a succinct little word as she grasped what had happened.

'Where are you?' she added, realising that Richard hadn't made a sound and terrified that he had been struck, until another streak of lightning silhouetted his long, leanly powerful body, turned towards the glass front of the foyer.

'The whole street is out on both sides, all the blocks,' he announced as darkness swallowed him again.

'Oh... Oh, the lift!' she absorbed. 'Luckily I'm only one floor up, if the lightning would just show me where the stairs start—yes, here we are!'

'Have you got any source of light up there? Gas lamps, a torch?'

'I'm not sure...candles,' she added vaguely.

'I'll come up with you.'

'OK,' she agreed, because it was very dark. 'Although we'll probably both break our necks. I've never used the stairs before. Where've you gone?'

'Here.' He was right behind her, and a moment later she felt his hand at her back. 'Ready? Wait a minute. How do you unlock your flat?'

'With an old-fashioned key,' she responded, understanding why he asked.

'Let's go, then.'

She could feel each individual finger and the thumb

and palm of his hand through the thin fabric of her clothes—no, it was as if the garments simply didn't exist! It induced an unmistakable breathlessness which was exacerbated rather than ameliorated when he changed his position and took hold of her upper arm.

'A few seconds later and we could have been trapped in the lift,' she observed with a giggle, trying to distract herself from the shock of too much sensation too suddenly.

'A situation rich with possibilities, but all way too conventional for someone like you, I imagine,' he returned mockingly.

'D'you think so?' Her breathing had grown even shallower as his comment activated her imagination.

'Oh, yes,' he confirmed whimsically. 'I think I see you as...a bit of an exhibitionist.'

'An exhibitionist?' she repeated with a funny little gasp. 'I am not!'

'An extrovert anyway, and, as you confessed earlier, you've never given much thought to what you're all about, so how would you know?' he challenged smoothly.

Maybe it was just the exertion of negotiating the stairs in the dark that was affecting her breathing. Challis tried to fool herself for a moment, but self-deception was no more her way than self-analysis, so she abandoned the attempt.

'There's a turn here,' she warned, and lightning flickered up from where it briefly filled the foyer below to prove her right.

They reached her flat without disaster, and Richard followed her in after she had unlocked the door.

'Where are these candles?' he asked abruptly.

'I'm not sure. Round and about.'

He was disgusted when he realised they were ornamental scented candles, scattered about her long, comfortable lounge.

'Don't you make any provision against emergencies such as this?' he deplored.

'I'm an optimist,' she claimed blithely, at ease again now that he was no longer touching her. 'Anyway, don't you think candles are romantic?'

She supposed she was flirting, just a little, but it didn't have to be reckless. They were too different to ever get romantically involved with each other, and as for finding the man sexually attractive—well, she was an adult and she could control her lust, couldn't she?

'Superfluously romantic,' Richard suggested, voice tight and hard with rejection.

That made it even safer. Challis gave him her warmest smile, liking the way his eyes reflected the flame of the candle burning in the prettily enamelled holder she had picked up.

'Let me give you something to drink?' she urged, turning for the kitchen. 'It's the least I can do after all your trouble—oh, I can't make coffee, though! I'm not sure what else there is. Let's see—no fridge light!'

She ignored the mildly exasperated look he gave her as he joined her in the kitchen.

'No wonder you were so insistent on your doggybag,' he drawled as her candle illuminated the interior of her little fridge, which contained three apples, two bottles of local spring water, still and sparkling, one small carton of milk and a bottle of champagne. 'I won't have anything to drink, thanks, Challis, but if you don't mind I'll hang around for a few minutes.

In case you haven't noticed, there's a cloudburst, and with the traffic lights out of commission, it'll be chaos out there. But this kind of downpour shouldn't last more than five or ten minutes, max.'

It was sheeting down by the sound of it, she registered belatedly.

'At least I've got an old battery radio, so we can have some music while you wait. Only it'll all be dinosaur rock for the stay-at-homes at this hour on a Saturday night—oh!' Challis broke off somewhat confusedly, eyeing him apologetically. 'But maybe you like it?'

'Being a dinosaur?' Richard prompted sardonically. 'There are other radio stations, you know.'

'Listen to the opposition? That's work,' she protested flippantly, although it was work she undertook regularly in the interests of staying competitive. 'If you won't have a drink, let's share my goodies. Go on, what would you like? Try one of these mozzarella and salami things.'

She had placed the candle on the kitchen's central work area to open the bag and now, impulsively, she lifted one of the exquisite snacks to his mouth to feed him, her painted nails shining and flickering with reflected candlelight. But something in Richard's attitude caused her to falter and finally lower her hand. He was motionless, his face seemingly carved from stone as he stared at her. Then contempt blazed in his eyes, visible even in the softness of candlelight.

In a dangerously soft voice, he said, 'You've decided I'm a better bet than Kel. Is that it, Challis?'

CHAPTER THREE

CHALLIS stared at Richard. She understood him perfectly, and her eyes were also blazing—with fury. The anger she felt should have been pure, but it was mixed with resentment and a distress that was inexplicable, considering that she was innocent of the charge.

She set her bag of goodies down on the counter.

'And what's led you to that conclusion? The romantic candlelight?' she suggested sarcastically.

Richard laughed, the sound low but harsh. 'That least of all, considering the way you had to search for a lighter. I guess you don't often have to resort to such scene-setting, looking and behaving the way you do. Most males will be easy prey.'

'But not you,' she snapped, more incensed than ever.

He watched her eat the little treat she had wanted to feed him. 'Did your scatty and scattered mind finally register that I control things with regard to Dovale Diamonds—that Kel is dependent on me and his mother for now? At least you like things clean enough to have broken up with Orchard before moving in, so it seems you do live by some rules, if only those which dictate that it's off with the old prior to on with the new... You know, I've been wondering what it was all about. I may have been a bit slow, stupidly giving you the benefit of the doubt. First there was the way you were coming on to me back there at that fling tonight, approaching me like that, all insouciant charm to begin with before the act slipped—'

'Coming on to you!' Challis had chewed and swallowed the morsel without tasting it. 'Don't flatter yourself. I was simply being friendly. Perhaps I thought you might be feeling out of place among so many music industry types.'

As she said it she realised how ridiculous it was to suggest anything of the sort to such an unfailingly self-assured man. He would be at ease in any company, however alien. Anyway, she had gone over to him on impulse, with nothing more than the idea of saying hello in her head.

'And then there's the way you've been flirting with me now,' he continued inexorably.

'What a complex you've got,' she snapped. 'In fact, I was just trying to provide you with a little of the fun that I imagine is missing from your life. I did try telling myself not to bother, but my mind must have kept on going—*mission, project*—without my even being aware of it... Oh, all right, maybe I was flirting a bit—'

'Yes, I'd begun to suspect. That's what you're really all about, isn't it? What you are? A chronic flirt. You'll even flirt with me.'

'Because it's part of the fun I'm talking about!'

'Your idea of fun, but not mine. Flirts are notoriously incapable of fidelity. They need whole squads of men.'

'But the issue of my being faithful to you or not is hardly in question here. I wasn't flirting with any designs on you, please believe me. You were admitting in the car that you keep making the mistake of taking me too seriously. Well, Richard, I don't take you seriously at all. I'm simply not interested. I'd never have any fun.'

'Empty fun,' he derided. 'I don't need it, so you can stop trying right now, Challis—if there's any truth in this explanation you're giving me.'

'Oh, I'll stop,' she returned scathingly. 'You're a lost cause.'

He just looked at her for the space of three seconds before turning for the kitchen door. 'I'll wait in your lounge.'

In no mood to let him escape when she had just thought of a few more things to say to him, she followed him into the lounge, around which they had left several candles burning.

'I suppose all this—this paranoia is because you've had less advantaged folk chasing after you for your money all your life,' she accused, coming to a halt as he stopped and faced her. 'And who can blame them? There's not much else there to attract.'

His sexy lips curved mockingly. 'Ah, an admission.'

'Except that I'm not interested in your diamonds, or the money they're worth,' she flared tempestuously, frustrated when a rolling blast of thunder forced her to wait before adding, 'But I hope someone does relieve you of the lot one of these fine days, because if you're so incapable of trusting anyone then you've had them way too long. You were born rich, weren't you? Dovale Diamonds has been in existence just about since diamonds were discovered here; I remember learning that at school. And you've been running the show since when? Your late teens or early twenties, I think I've read somewhere. Did your parents have the savvy to realise how it might twist them and hand it over to you as soon as you were old enough?'

'They died when I was thirteen,' he told her expressionlessly. 'They were drowned at sea. A yachting accident.'

'Oh...Richard, I'm sorry!' Challis was instantly contrite. 'I didn't know. I just thought they must be very private people because the media never mention them—and yet I suppose I must have heard.'

'How could you? You'd have been a tiny kid at the time it happened, barely able to talk,' he allowed easily, and actually smiled. 'Although that's hard to imagine.'

'It must still be referred to occasionally, though. I should have known.' She wanted to reach out and touch him, partly in apology but more in sympathy. 'Thirteen? Oh, that's hard; it's so horribly young to lose both parents—and you'll have had the added pressure of being heir to Dovale Diamonds.'

Richard shrugged dismissively. 'I've survived. But it probably turned me into a very *serious* kid overnight. A dirty word in your language, right? What were you like as a little girl?'

They were both still on their feet, and she was momentarily distracted by the way his eyes alternately reflected the candlelight and the lightning still flickering and blazing outside.

Then she laughed a little awkwardly, still ashamed of her insensitivity, especially when he was being generous enough not to make a big issue of it.

'A brat, in all probability. My folks were always fighting, so I'd join in. Between us, my dad and I gave my poor mom a hard time; we were always so hellbent on doing our own thing... I'm lucky, I've still got them both—living out in the Magaliesberg since they sort of retired. Dad still gets to play his saxophone with the guys occasionally, and mom does a bit of freelance bookkeeping.'

'All of which tells me more about your parents than it does about you, so come over here,' he invited, holding out a hand.

The unexpectedly indulgent tone had her responding instinctively, actually taking a couple of steps towards him. Then she stopped, startled. That wasn't lightning or even candlelight she could see lighting the deep golden eyes now; it came from the man himself, the gleam and glow of a mood, warm and overtly sensual.

'Why?' she demanded bluntly.

He smiled at her. 'When you wanted to shake hands the other morning you said touching was important, it enables you to learn something about the other person. So let's get to know each other, Challis.'

'*What?*' Astonishment at this volte-face lifted her voice. 'Richard, a minute ago you were objecting to my flirting and now... What do you need to know anyway? I thought you'd decided you know it all already, what my motives are, what I am!'

His smile had turned slightly crooked, and almost rueful, she noticed.

'Yes, only every little once in a while something seeps through, a warmth, a *niceness,* that makes me wonder if I've got it wrong. If I've got you wrong.'

It was engagingly self-deprecating, and once again the readiness with which he admitted to a possible error was surprising, coming from a man who was generally the opposite of open about himself.

Won over, Challis sent him one of her happiest smiles. 'Have I got you wrong too?'

'Probably.'

'Only in some ways. In others I'm sure I—'

'One thing I've definitely got right about you—you talk far too much!'

Then he had her in his arms, and she liked it. No, she loved it, her own arms sliding eagerly round the hardness of his body and hugging tightly.

His lips were so warm, nudging at hers, advancing and retreating in a series of teasing, tasting little kisses. Hungrily, she took him further into her mouth, kissing his lower lip, holding it between both of hers. Then she shivered as he deepened the exploration and she surrendered to the erotic probing of his tongue, her own as sensually questing.

Deep in the pit of her body a throbbing sensation began, as if a partner to her heart were beating down there, where she was most sensitively receptive. It was like a slow storm, and she stirred languidly against the taut length of his body as his lips slipped caressingly from her mouth to her jaw and on to the smoothness of her neck. A hand at her shoulder, skilful fingers brushing aside the soft material of her unfastened jacket, and then his mouth in the curve between her neck and shoulder.

Challis shuddered helplessly as he kissed her there, delicious, conventional outward kisses, followed by the inward, pulling kind, so intrinsically intimate, heating her blood, turning her flesh so hot that she felt as if she were in a fever.

She wanted him! It wasn't a thought, it wasn't any kind of intellectual realisation. Instead it was a recognition made by her most fundamental senses as he sucked sensually at her skin and his hands found their sure way beneath her loose jacket, fingers splaying possessively over her midriff.

'Richard...' She could barely articulate his name.

There was an ocean of desire in the hollow of her womanhood, rocking, rolling waves of it, a liquid, gently turbulent sensation that could lead to total abandonment if kept up too long—to a kind of mindless yet wholly voluntarily drowning—in torment or delight? She sensed that, and yet she didn't want it to stop. She wanted more, all of him, and in obedience to the wish her hands slid to the lapels of the jacket he still wore, intent on its removal.

'That's enough!'

The sharp denial came as a shock, leaving her too stunned to resist as he released her and freed himself. They stared at each other with darkened eyes, both breathing unevenly.

'You're going to blame me, aren't you?' she guessed tartly, in response to his hard, accusing expression. 'What will it be? My behaviour? Or are we back to the way I look?'

'Not you. Me.' Richard raked his fingers through his dark hair and expelled an angry breath. 'I must be losing my mind. You... But you were just being your natural self, while I— No! I won't let myself be suckered, seduced by a compulsive flirt. I can resist you.'

There was an insult in there somewhere, but Challis wasn't ready to let herself think about it—about any of this—yet. She shaped a blazing, blistering smile.

'You shouldn't say things like that to me, Richard. I might take it as a challenge. I would, if you were different.'

His eyes glittered—nothing to do with shortening candles or receding lightning.

'Different in what way?'

Wounded herself, she went for the jugular. 'Younger. Looser.'

'Looser?' The repetition was disdainful.

'Less uptight. *My* kind of man.'

'And even if I were,' he offered deliberately, 'I could still resist you, because I do not trust you, and I would not trust you a proverbial inch until you'd proved yourself otherwise.'

'Academic,' she drawled dismissively. 'You see, I'm not interested in proving anything to you. Like I say, you're just too different. The whole thing is a turn-off. It's all very apt, though. Isn't a diamond supposed to be the hardest substance in the world?'

'The hardest naturally occurring substance.' He understood her perfectly. 'You're pretty ruthless yourself. But you seemed quite enthusiastic about the things the other morning.'

'You don't fit any of the nicer diamond clichés. For instance, have you heard the phrase "Crazy diamond"—someone who lives life on the edge, takes risks? Now *those* might keep you warm at night.'

'So I'm not reckless enough for you?'

'You're not exactly what some people call a "diamond geezer" either—a regular good guy,' she mourned facetiously, thinking how strange it was that they should suddenly be co-operating with each other like this, engaging in this flip little exchange, lightening the atmosphere.

Richard's eyes glinted, as if he had caught the stray thought, and he smiled, the charm of it unrestrained, making her heart clench and the breath catch in her throat.

'Let's just say—well, we don't need to part enemies, do we? Only I think we do have to part—' He broke off as the street lights outside came on, and Challis moved to press the wall switch, illuminating the lounge, making the candles look pallid and pathetic. 'Electricity and sanity restored. The rain is easing too, so I'll go now. Thanks is all I can honestly say, Challis.'

'For what?' she asked, feeling suddenly flat, resenting the light now flooding the lounge, too bright somehow, although she used pastel-tinted bulbs in a soft shade of pink.

'For leaving Kel alone, if nothing else.' Richard moved towards the door which led into the flat's high-ceilinged entrance hall, but he stopped as he reached it. 'Challis? How much did you have to drink tonight?'

'Because of the way I was behaving earlier?' She guessed what had inspired the question. 'I was high on a good mood, nothing else. That's kind of spoilt now.'

'I know.' He sounded almost regretful as he touched her jaw lightly, his face tightening as she jerked her head away. 'We don't match at all, do we?'

'Clash is more like it,' she muttered grudgingly.

His eyes held hers, intently probing. 'Truly just a good mood? Because you're coming down unnaturally hard and fast.'

'Is that what you believe of me?'

'You move on the fringes of a milieu in which intoxication is not totally unknown,' he pointed out coolly.

'I've told you before. I'm not part of the music business; I'm in the media. Try listening to our station some time. We're unequivocally anti-drugs.' Challis was neutrally unemphatic, grown too used to this particular perception of her world to let it bother her unduly.

'Hypocrisy from the media isn't totally unknown either,' Richard suggested calmly.

That was what bothered her. His inability to accept anything she said for what it was worth, his distrust as hard as one of his diamonds.

'You just don't understand me.'

She made it tiredly comical, but the fact of it was central to her unaccustomed feeling of depression. In the end, despite some promising chinks, she had got nowhere with this man. He was no closer to knowing her.

'Either that, or I understand you all too well,' he retorted with faint humour. 'Goodbye, Challis. It's been—interesting, knowing you.'

But he hadn't known her, and there would be no further opportunities for him to do so, she accepted after he had gone. And yet she had let the thing go too far, she decided as she locked the door and returned to the lounge, blowing out the now superfluous candles one by one.

She had been reckless after all, considering the extent of her desire for him, but she simply hadn't anticipated how actually being in his arms would affect her, despite having found him attractive before.

Oh, well, it wouldn't happen again, and the regret she was feeling was simply because she was used to being liked and trusted, and was usually capable of winning over those who started out with preconceived reservations. It wasn't as if she wanted anything more from Richard Dovale, however sexy he was. An affair in which the partners couldn't talk to each other without disagreeing wasn't her idea of fun, and any sort of involvement with Richard, even the briefest kind, would just be a fight. She had grown up in the midst of one long, unending quarrel, emerging happily unscathed herself but all too conscious of how destructive such conflict could be to the main protagonists. No way was she looking for a version of that relationship for herself.

'Miles wants to see you,' Nicki Adams, the station's receptionist and general Girl Friday announced, when Challis arrived at the small Sounds FM building early on Monday afternoon to prepare for that night's show, having come straight from the brunch with which she usually started her working day in one or other of Rosebank's cafés.

'Brett Case has landed a part in a local soap opera,' Miles announced when she went through to his office. 'His contract with us has an immediate release clause. Zora has done a full year on the production side, plus plenty of graveyard shifts, as well as sitting in for the rest of you, so I'm going to give her his slot, but it means we'll need to take on a new trainee. And are you remembering that Angelo leaves to take up his American scholarship in a few months' time?'

'Remembering? It haunts my dreams!' Challis claimed melodramatically, since Angelo Goliath was their star DJ.

'So, whoever we train will probably end up taking over from him.'

'What do you suggest? Juggling while we run another competition, inviting all the wannabes out there to send in tapes?'

'I already know who we need,' Miles stated, and her heart fell. 'Because if he's going to replace Angelo, he is going to have to be dynamite—which Kel Sheridan is, on that demo he sent you.'

'Oh, no, Miles,' Challis protested faintly. 'It'll cause trouble in the family if we go for him.'

'Which is precisely what we're going to do. And to hell with the family.'

'Miles, we can't!' Just the thought of Richard Dovale's reaction was distressing.

'I can, if you won't. I'm still running this show, you know,' he added crisply. The reminder that, while he was her friend and mentor, he was still also her boss caused her to flush, although he adopted a gentler tone as he went on. 'But by the time he replaces Angelo you will in all probability be doing so, if things work out for me. You've shocked me, Challis. Don't you want the best for Sounds?'

'Of course I do. I'm sorry, Miles, I'm being unprofessional, aren't I?' she acknowledged readily, ashamed of the lapse and knowing exactly who she had to blame for it. 'Kel Sheridan is perfect for our needs, and as he's eighteen it has nothing to do with his uncle, his mother, his father, his pet goldfish or anyone else.'

'Now that's much more like you, Challis!' Miles applauded. 'That's settled, then, and as it was essentially you who attracted him to us in the first place, and he'll ultimately be your *wunderkind,* I thought I'd give you the opportunity to make him the offer; there's no way he's going to refuse if his past persistence is any indication. Hell, you never know, you might even be able to ease things with regard to the family, as you seem to know something about the situation and you're obviously concerned about it. Right! Set up another meeting, talk to him, and then, if he's what we hope, bring him in and we'll show him a contract... Or should I come along again?'

'No, I can handle it,' Challis decided.

Richard was a very private man, and he would hate it if any family matters came up when she met Kel and a stranger was present—although why she should be so specifically ready to consider his feelings was a mystery, apart from her general reluctance to cause distress to anyone.

She told Miles about Serle's behaviour on Saturday night, and went away to call Kel Sheridan in private. This time she got him in person, instead of just his recorded voice, at the number he had supplied. When he understood that she wanted to meet him, he fizzed with even more enthusiasm than she was accustomed to hearing when he called in to her show. He tried to keep her talking after the time and place were arranged, but she cut him off and settled down to study her faxes and E-mail, which was always her first task during the couple of afternoon hours she put into programming her show.

'I can't believe I'm actually meeting you at last!' Kel repeated when they met the following morning, at the same coffee shop at which Challis had expected him the previous week.

Seen close up, he was a young version of his uncle, with the same dramatic colouring, and almost as desperately good-looking, and yet he failed to flutter her pulses. Just a little too young, as Richard had been too old, she decided, with a can't-win smile, but his personal appearances and club gigs would be a riot.

'This is professional,' she cautioned him coolly.

'Can't it be personal too?'

'Sorry,' she drawled, but smiling widely, too practised in dealing with such advances to overstate.

'Then I'll hide my broken heart and accept the professional,' he announced easily but excitedly, obviously confident of what this was about.

'Do you have a job at present?' she asked him.

'No, but I will have in another minute if this is what I think it is,' he stated euphorically, and she had to laugh.

'Looks like it,' she conceded laconically.

'I have to start out on the technical and production side, right? Will I get to work with you?'

'Me and Angelo Goliath.' Her eyes sparkled, full of challenging mockery. 'It's going to foul up your social life, isn't it? A six-hour shift from nineteen hundred hours to one in the morning, plus extra most weekends?'

'Hey, I'd take a vow of celibacy to work with you, learn from you!' Kel declared fervently.

They talked about radio work and music for a while. Then, during a pause, Challis sent him a sweetly malicious smile.

'Did you get that tan in Mauritius last week?'

'How do you know about that?' He was badly startled.

'Uncle Richard.' Strangely, she had some difficulty saying the name as lightly as she had intended.

Kel clapped a hand over his eyes, the gesture somewhat affected. 'I wasn't going to mention the connection. But how the hell do you know him?'

'It's not important.' She didn't want to exacerbate whatever conflict lay between uncle and nephew by telling the latter about Richard's attempt to interfere. 'But he doesn't want you working in radio, does he?'

He sighed resignedly. 'That's for my mother's sake. She doesn't, and he tries to take care of her. I admire the guy for that. He always has, even when he was a kid, she says, although she was four years older, and now he's even letting us live in the guest cottage in his grounds until she decides what to do. My father took off five years ago—for overseas, we think—so she finally divorced him and sold the house we had. But then she went into one of those phases when she can't bring herself to make decisions. Richard is cool. He understands what a bore it is for me, having her clinging to me, so he had the cottage altered so I could lead my own life, or a semblance of it: my own separate entrance and all that, even an extra phone installed just for me. In return, I'm supposed to refrain from upsetting her too much and, well, she's my mother, so I oblige most of the time. That's why I went to Mauritius with her... But this is my life, my future, and it has nothing to do with them.'

'Of course it hasn't.' Challis was in full agreement there, but it didn't stop her sympathising with Richard, who was obviously just trying to protect his sister. 'Well, break the news to them gently, like the mature, together young adult a Sounds FM DJ is supposed to be... Now! D'you want to come and meet Miles Logan?'

'Just a minute! I want to talk to you.'

Richard Dovale!

Challis spun round in the entrance of the squat little

Sounds FM building, the skirt of her soft midnight-blue dress swirling about her.

She was dressed for outside work, her radio show merely the filling in the sandwich tonight, since she had come straight from a personal appearance and still had to honour an agreement to put in a brief appearance at a club after her show ended. It was a venue notoriously short of parking, which was why Serle Orchard had just dropped her off. She had been disgusted when he had approached her at the newly opened shopping mall half an hour ago, just as she'd been about to phone for the second of the four taxis she planned to use that evening. He had been insistent that he had to talk to her.

'No time—unless you drive me to work and talk while you're doing it,' she had told him shortly, afraid that he might try and delay her if she refused outright. And such was his anxiety as to whether she had told anyone about his attempt to bribe her that he had agreed, although she had regretted the suggestion when he'd become verbally abusive after she had admitted to informing Miles.

Now here was another man insisting that he wanted to talk to her, and with no more friendliness than Serle had shown.

'Talk? I don't think so,' she shot back at Richard sceptically.

He looked too angry for anything so civilised as talking, the amber eyes blazing as lethally as those of an enraged jungle creature. Once again he was wearing a suit, but that did nothing to mute an air of danger, especially as he wasn't quite as immaculate as usual. His tie had been loosened a little and his dark, swept back hair looked as if he had raked his fingers through it. Somehow it made him appear even sexier—and deadly, because it suggested that his control wasn't absolute.

'Talk,' he repeated relentlessly, 'and you know what about.'

'And there I was, thinking we'd got away with it,' she regretted flippantly, smiling at the inside security guard who had approached on seeing Richard follow her into the reception area. 'It's all right, I know him.'

Oh, yes, she knew what this was about. The savagery with which his gaze scorched her vivacious face, unsoftened by any appreciation of her shiny red mouth and the sleek, inverted-tulip fall of her gleaming blue-black hair, would have told her if her conscience hadn't. He was intent on much more than a warning against Serle Orchard this time, although he must have seen him drop her off, as it seemed he had been waiting for her.

Kel Sheridan was due to start work on Monday. This was Friday night. Despite her irritation with Serle, she had arrived at Sounds full of her usual enthusiasm. Now, unexpectedly, she found that doubled. Confronted by Richard, she felt alive, exhilarated, even knowing why he was here.

She had missed him! Incredible! How could you miss someone you had only met twice?

'I've just got back from a business trip to a couple of our mines to find my nephew ready to go to work for you next week and my sister consequently in need of sedation,' Richard grated, truly looking and sounding as if he hated her.

Challis glanced round. Only the guard was present, Nicki having gone home hours ago.

'Come in here,' she invited Richard, opening the

door to Miles's office, knowing it would be empty as he worked conventional hours. 'But I should warn you I haven't got much time. I go on air at ten, but I need to be in the studio before that.'

'You lied to me,' he accused implacably as she faced him after closing the door. 'I should have known. Promises mean nothing to someone like you.'

Dear God, the way his eyes were glittering!

'I think you took too much for granted.' She spoke sharply, a little unnerved. 'I only promised to think about what you said, and you yourself have called it a nebulous promise.'

'The first time we met, it was,' he allowed, but ruthlessly somehow. 'Last Saturday night you were coming across as if you'd made a definite decision to leave Kel alone. Hell, you even seemed to make a virtue of it, as if you believed you deserved praise.'

'I thought I had decided,' she admitted honestly, and spread her hands expressively. 'I was wrong. I was wrong to promise what I did. It was unprofessional of me, and I don't think I've ever been unprofessional before. I don't know why I did it. I shouldn't have.'

'You actually temporarily forgot to put your own interests first?' he taunted mercilessly.

'The station's.'

He spent a second or two absorbing the correction. 'You don't recognise that professionalism, while admirable in itself, might occasionally be circumscribed by moral or ethical considerations?'

'I did nothing immoral or unethical—and you know it,' Challis said abruptly, very sure of that.

'Apart from lulling me into a false sense of security.'

She smiled caustically. 'It seems to me it's Kel's mother who's the insecure one. But if she doesn't like it, if you don't like it, talk to Kel. He must deal with it, or cave in and not deal with it, as the case may be. It's nothing to do with me. I'm not part of the family—hallelujah!'

'Yes, it's that easy for you,' Richard accepted disgustedly. 'You're not involved. The rest of us are. But the worst of it is the way I feel so betrayed. I was beginning to believe in you.'

CHAPTER FOUR

CHALLIS tried to swallow, afraid of the hot, smarting sensation around her eyes. The emotion catching at her heart and constricting her throat was both unexpected and unwelcome.

That personal candour of Richard's again!

How could she defend her position when he disarmed her with such openness?

Not that he wasn't still angry, but she felt this as a setback without ever having been aware that she had gained any ground to begin with. Well, he despised her now. Look at the cruel twist to those sexy lips and the contempt hardening his beautiful eyes!

'Richard, I'm sorry—' With an indrawn breath she arrested it right there, bright, tender lower lip caught between her teeth as she reminded herself that she had little to apologise for. 'Yes, well, maybe I'm sorry if there's trouble in the family, but, to be honest, your sister's reaction to Kel's contract sounds a bit hysterical to me. If you're not exaggerating.'

'I'm not.'

Still distraught, and with a feeling that she might have revealed some weakness, she flashed him a blastingly defiant smile and steeled herself to be unkind.

'Then she sounds like the traditional possessive mother, trying to dictate her little darling's life and resorting to emotional blackmail when he shows signs of having a mind of his own. But her little boy is a big one now, all of eighteen and legal in every way.'

She saw the hostility that made a rigid mask of Richard's face but she carried on recklessly. 'Don't you think she should be encouraged to face up to reality?'

'She's faced far too much reality in her life already.' He rejected the suggestion tautly.

'With you there to protect her?' she mocked sceptically. 'Though I don't know why you think she—and Kel by extension—is your responsibility, going around trying to interfere in their affairs like this. She's his mother, she's an adult—she's actually older than you too, isn't she?'

'And when I didn't interfere, when I didn't say anything nearly twenty years ago, I let her in for the most hellish marriage on earth—a marriage she has only just terminated, although the bastard disappeared five years ago when she finally found the strength to refuse to finance his self-indulgence any longer.' The bitter self-reproach was shocking. 'You're too young to remember Haigh Sheridan, aren't you? He was a local actor, not a very successful one, but it was all he was prepared to do, and he did get some work in radio theatre—yes, Challis, radio!

'He knew what Lucinda would be worth after our parents were drowned and he made sure it was to him that she turned for comfort, and he made sure of *her* by getting her pregnant. I could see what was happening, what he was after—the financial freedom to pursue his pathetic career in comfort—but I was bloody thirteen years old. I couldn't attempt to guide her; she wouldn't have listened to me anyway. She didn't listen to our trustees and guardians. As you say, she was my big sister, four years older than me. But I knew her. I knew her need for a settled, conventional

life, devoid of surprises and upheavals, and she wasn't
going to get that with someone as restless as Haigh.

'So it proved, and worse, because he hid from his
lack of talent and other inadequacies in a bottle—
much as he sought to find a more typically showbiz
image of himself in other women's beds. He disappeared several times, but that was preferable to the
physical and emotional abuse he inflicted on her when
he was around, although Lucinda spent years trying
to cover it up... And when I look at her now, see
what has become of her and remember what was done
to her, I wish I'd tried, I *wish* I'd said something. And
when I see her terror at the idea of Kel *becoming* his
father... It's not for Kel, any of this. I'd let him make
his own mistakes, that's my inclination where most
adults are concerned, but my sister is a vulnerable
woman.'

Distress darkened Challis's eyes. Her heart went
out to the boy he had been, wise and wanting to take
an adult's responsibility, but with his age against him.

'Richard—' She didn't know what to say.

'It's all right,' he allowed reluctantly, registering
her expression. 'You didn't know.'

'I'm too ready with my mouth,' she admitted con-
tritely.

The look he gave her, and her bright mouth specifically, was eloquent. 'Lippy.'

'Before I'm in possession of the facts.' Wryly.

'Well, you know now.' His attitude had hardened
again.

'Yes, and oddly enough I'm familiar with the scenario. In a way, it's my parents all over again—although my dad only drinks socially and has never
abused Mom. But he's a jazz musician—he also used

to do quite a bit of radio work—and she's a book-keeper. She's a conformist, she craves order, a cheque for the same amount every month—but he must follow trends, the guys and his muse, and go where the music is hottest and coolest.'

'And you're more his child than hers,' Richard understood harshly.

That was why he and she could never get together, however attracted to each other they might be, and she thought he *was* grudgingly attracted to her. It would be yet another version of the same story, only with the sexes reversed.

She twitched a shoulder. 'We DJs may not be conventional people, but we're not all as bad as this guy Haigh, you know. I don't think Kel is going to turn into him.'

'Try telling Lucinda that.'

'I will, if you think it'll help.' Challis was half serious.

'Lord, no! Stay away from her! It'll only make her even more frightened if she knows Kel's getting mixed up with someone like you.'

'Thanks.' Sarcastically, but then, with greater sincerity, 'I'm not Sounds FM, you know. It's the *station* he's coming to work for.'

'You're a primary attraction.'

'There's nothing I can do about that.'

The stark disbelief that kept his expression unyielding had her heart dropping towards her stomach.

'For God's sake!' His right hand made a fist, pumping downward to give emphasis to his frustration and anger. 'Do you think I like having to do this? Coming after you and telling you our private family business?

I hate it, especially as I can see your point of view, and Kel's, but there's my sister.'

The sister he hadn't been able to protect at thirteen. Challis lowered her eyes while she hardened her heart.

'Kel has a vocation.' She felt a bit embarrassed, phrasing it that way, but she didn't know how else to put it.

'He's influenced by you.' Then, as he discarded all control, his hand shot up and out to grasp her shoulder, long fingers flexing and biting into her. 'What do I have to do? How do I make you talk him out of it?'

Unrestrained anger vibrated in his voice and darkened his face. Challis lifted her own hand, slapping it warningly over the back of his where it still curled insistently round her shoulder.

'You can't,' she told him sharply, but found herself incapable of adding to it as she realised that her hand was lingering over his, fingers straying to the back of his wrist, involuntarily stroking.

She stared at his mouth, the wrong thing to do if she wanted to free herself from what was nothing more or less than sexual fascination.

Dismayed, she understood that Richard knew exactly what was happening. The angry frustration that had blazed in his eyes was giving way to a heated golden gleam, fatal in its sensuality, although the smile he gave her was calculating.

'What and how?' he repeated, but softly now, in a tone of diabolical awareness, as if he finally saw his way. 'How to get you to undo what you've done? You're attracted to me, aren't you? Shall I use that, enslave you, persuade you that way—and have you in return for my trouble?'

She was the angry one now, laughing scornfully.

'Men don't *have* women. We'll have each other, or we won't have anything at all.'

'Suits me,' Richard drawled, his smile grown bitingly derisive. 'Although if this attraction were all it was I would resist it, because there isn't a single other thing we've got in common—'

'You said it!'

'But as I have something else to gain...' He left the rest of it unspoken as he lowered his head, his arms sliding round her to form a prison for her slender body.

'You're rapidly relinquishing whatever remote chance you might have had of gaining anything,' Challis snapped, more insulted than she had ever been in her life. Although she understood that anger drove him and he wouldn't normally be talking—behaving—like this.

'And of having you?' he prompted audaciously, because her body was arching helplessly up to his as her arms closed round him and she had let her head fall back, wanting his kiss, the kiss he continued to deny her as he went on in a musingly contemptuous tone, 'You called yourself an optimist the other night, and I have to believe it if you live in perpetual expectation of an opportunity to...give yourself. As you must if you're so beautifully dressed—dressed to seduce—even coming in to work in a radio studio.'

'I was invited to make a cameo at the opening of that new shopping mall in the north. Personal appearances are part of my job, although they had some big banker doing the speech. They had fireworks,' she added inconsequentially, but with a reminiscent sparkle of pleasure brightening her dark blue eyes.

'Ah, you like fireworks, do you?' Unexpected humour intensified the gleam in his. 'Why doesn't that surprise me?'

Now she was stroking the back of his neck, Challis discovered distractedly.

'I suppose you think they're dangerous?' she taunted, knowing she had to stop this, and fast. 'Oh, they are really, but a controlled display, done by an expert in pyrotechnics, that's all right.'

'That's not how you like sex, is it? A safe, controlled display, nothing reckless, no unexpected flashes or explosions?'

She decided it was time to make herself clear. 'You'll never know, will you?'

'Because you're like a firework yourself,' he continued fancifully.

'A Catherine wheel?' she suggested, out of sheer vanity since she liked them, intrigued because no one else had ever interrupted an attempted seduction to talk to her like this—tease her like this.

'Named after a particularly cruel contraption, so inapt in several ways.'

'A rocket, then?'

She was flirting with the man again! What was wrong with her? They didn't even have a five-minute future together, so why encourage him?

'There are similarities, but, no. One of those maddening crackers that fizz and bang and never jump the way you expect them to,' he decided wickedly. 'Now those are definitely dangerous.'

She gave him a slow, devastating smile. 'So back off.'

'No.'

And, help her, she didn't want him to. He was kissing her now, and caressing her, his lips and hands everywhere. The warmth of his mouth, brushing over her lips, skimming her jaw, probing the delicate hollow at the base of her throat, was a thrill like no other she had ever known. She chased his mouth with her own, hungering for something more substantial, until he too tired of such playful skirmishing. Then a deeper pleasure surged and sucked at her as his mouth opened over hers and invaded it, hotly erotic.

His hands still moved all over her, in her hair, about her back, waist and hips, at her thighs, and Challis trembled in a delirium of sweet sensation, pressing her body up to his in unaffected expression of the desire he was feeding so skilfully. Her own hands were at his head, fingers plunging into the thick dark hair to keep him there, kissing her like this for ever.

Their two mouths were one, separating occasionally only to collide instantly again, lips and tongues ceaselessly, passionately questing. Vaguely, distantly, Challis understood that it was she who was making those soft sounds of helpless delight as Richard's hands found their sure way up under the gossamer-light skirt of her short floaty dress to cup her neat, firm buttocks. His fingers drifted sensitively beneath the edge of her panties, the astonishing tenderness with which they stroked the satiny skin there a new thrill.

She could feel his manhood hardening, rising and raging against the clothes which were all that lay between them as he moved her back against the desk, half lifting her on to it. She couldn't be still, all turbulent motion, writhing, undulating, arching and rubbing herself luxuriously against him. Her mouth was wild and wet under his, and she didn't need his hands moving round to her straining thighs to part them. She was doing it for him, legs eagerly drawing him into their wanton embrace, her body taut and shuddering, just as his was.

Something dug into the back of her waist as she was pressed back against the desk. Then it was displaced with a small clatter. It was Miles Logan's desk phone, and she grasped where she was and what was happening with something similar to the shock of jumping out of a bad dream and then thinking it was real after all.

It wasn't enough to dull her body's craving for the magnificent, dark, golden-eyed creature bent over her like a promise or a threat. She had to force herself to think, to focus on the things Richard had said before they had got on to fireworks, to remember what this was really about.

She got her hands to his shoulders and pushed.

'No. We are not having each other on my boss's desk.' She was gasping slightly as she made her legs slacken their hold on him, but she was forcefully articulate. 'He wouldn't like it, I wouldn't like it and, while I don't know you well enough to be sure, I don't think you'd like it—or you wouldn't when it was done. Not conventional enough for someone who wears suits all the time.'

'Conventional,' Richard repeated, sounding more irritated than anything else as he stepped back.

Challis let out a huge sigh of relief. It wasn't that she had been afraid of his ignoring her protest, though. No, it was her own weakness that had scared her so badly. A few more seconds' physical contact and she would have been debilitatingly in thrall to his mind-swamping sensuality, clinging and trying to convince him that she hadn't meant it.

Fatal. Richard Dovale and her—it just wouldn't do, wouldn't work for a minute. Different worlds, she reminded herself. They were diametric opposites in every way.

Eyes still darkened and glazed, she stared at him, and was finally able to get her flushed and swollen lips into the shape of a smile.

'I guess we're quits.' She managed to make it lightly dismissive, with only the slightest quiver of underlying reproach. 'If you came here feeling betrayed, I'm the one who's disappointed now—let down! Even if you don't respect me, I'd have thought you'd respect yourself too much to resort to using sex to—to persuade me!'

The condemnation tightened his face, she noted. She was still perched on the edge of Miles's desk, and he watched her cross her ankles, slender above her neat feet encased in pretty blue shoes. Then he met her eyes, the expression in his complicated.

'I apologise. It was a bit over the top, wasn't it?' he conceded quietly, and shrugged. 'I was angry. I'll have to think of something else.'

'Like bribing me with one of your diamonds?' she suggested flippantly, unable to resist finding out how seriously he would take the joke. 'No deal. Now if you were to raise the offer to one of your actual mines…'

'Joke. Very funny. You see, I'm beginning to know you,' he added complacently. 'No, your weaknesses lie in the area of physical pleasures. Sex and food, preferably scrounged, are the ones I know about so far.'

'But I won't let the station down or compromise my professionalism for either, so you'll have to do better than that, genius,' Challis quipped. 'Except that nothing you can come up with will make any difference. What is it you and your sister think Kel ought to be doing with his life anyway? Something at Dovale Diamonds, I suppose?'

He stirred impatiently. 'Lucinda has ideas of that sort. I don't care. He'll inherit her share, but he doesn't have to actually get personally involved if he doesn't want to. She hasn't. I don't care what he does, as long as it's well away from the kind of thing she's so frightened of—entertainment, radio, the rest of it.'

She shook her head angrily. 'But don't you and she see? You can't try to control people, mould them into versions of yourselves. I know! My mother tried, and she made my father miserable, me miserable, and herself miserable. Some people aren't made for safe, stable routine.'

Her voice had taken on the unmistakable ring of sincerity, of one desperately trying to help, but Richard seemed unmoved by it, a challenging glint appearing in his eyes.

'You, for instance? Does that make us incompatible?'

'We were talking about your nephew,' she snapped.

'Why does his happiness concern you if you're not interested in him on a personal level? Or can't you make up your mind between him and Serle Orchard? That *was* who brought you to work, wasn't it? Why are you back with him anyway? Because you've realised I won't play now you've gone back on your word about Kel? Because flirts like you need whole battalions of men to keep them happy?'

'I don't have that kind of ego problem!'

'Who said anything about a problem? You're problem-free; you've told me you don't let things bother you. No, it's just the way you are. A flirt.'

And his look told her how much he deplored that.

'If that's what you want to believe, go ahead, because even if you were right I wouldn't extend my flirting to a man like you—someone who refuses to have faith in anything I say!'

Trust was important, and his lack of it actually hurt, although she knew she was stupid to let it.

'Even if the evidence points another way?'

'Yes! When it's only *seeming* evidence. Then I expect to be given the benefit of the doubt.'

'All the same, we're attracted to each other, you and I.' Considering how angry he had been about her supposed influence over Kel, this conversation was incongruous. 'I hope you're not going to be coy and deny it.'

'I'm never coy!' Challis flared, and gave him a slashing smile. 'Of course I'm attracted to you. If we had a single other thing in common, I'd be in hot pursuit—or if I believed in the sort of quick affair where lust is all that's necessary because it's only going to last five minutes.'

He laughed, a silkily sensual sound that made her skin prickle.

'Five minutes, Challis? I'm better than that.'

It activated her imagination and heated her blood.

'I'll bet,' she said shortly.

'And so are you.'

'Thanks for the vote of confidence, but, as we've agreed, we've got zilch in common. Incompatible is right, and then some.'

'So what's the solution?' he enquired, clearly deriving some kind of idle amusement from the debate, a fact which surprised her. 'A brief run-its-course fling would seem to be the obvious one, only you've just said—unpredictably—that you don't believe in them, and I'm not really into them either—predictably, I'm sure you feel?'

'Well, yes,' she admitted with an apologetic little grin, slightly astonished to discover that she was actually beginning to enjoy herself. 'So there is no solution.'

'And you'll settle for my nephew, with whom you have a lot in common, even if your hormones are urging you in my direction?' he taunted.

It spoilt her fun. The man really was incapable of trust if he still seriously suspected her of being after Kel on a personal level.

'He looks a lot like you, and he's closer to me in age. He's also unexpectedly mature in some ways, which helps narrow the little gap there is,' she offered naughtily, looking at her watch and sliding off the desk in a hurry, after righting Miles's phone. 'The time! Sorry, I have to move it. You'd better go too.'

As she whirled past Richard to open the office door she caught a last glimpse of his dark face, and had to swallow a gasp of shock. He looked so very, very angry, absolutely furious, his earlier rage negligible by comparison.

She fled, not out of cowardice but in obedience to the demands of her job, trying to appease her conscience as she went. The man didn't deserve reassurance when he consistently failed to accept her word. She had already told him she wasn't interested in Kel, so he ought to know she had been joking.

Briefly it occurred to her that his fury might have

something to do with sexual jealousy, but she couldn't really believe that was it. Hadn't he boasted that he could and would resist her in the absence of anything else to achieve?

She had thought she could resist him equally well and, reflecting on what had happened to her once she was in his arms, she felt angry with herself for having been so over-confident. It had never happened to her before, this inability to control the attraction she felt. It was because he was older, she supposed, sensually skilled and sophisticated.

When she reached her studio her friend and colleague, Zora Molefe, serving her last night as producer, had a message from Kel. 'Call him at home when you can tonight. He sat in on the first half of Angelo's show to check out what I do. Hey, you look—all loved up!'

Challis grimaced, wishing she had stopped off to fix her face in the cloakroom. 'Love had nothing to do with it, I promise you.'

'C'mon, Challis! We all know you believe in love.'

'Yes, well, that's the trouble,' Challis retorted cryptically.

Because if only she didn't believe in love, she thought she might just go ahead and jump into an affair with Richard Dovale—assuming he should be willing—incompatibility notwithstanding.

Challis found the opportunity to call Kel half an hour into her show, after announcing four songs in a row.

'Challis?' Kel was full of enthusiasm. 'Did Zora tell you what it's about? Party at my place tomorrow night for those of you I've met so far, and then a club or three, to celebrate her promotion and my new job. What do you say?'

Set foot on Richard's property? Silently Challis contemplated the pros and cons. Too many of the cons seemed to be for Richard's sake, and she decided he was no longer deserving of her consideration.

'I'm in.'

'Great! Challis—oh, hi,' he digressed as he was obviously interrupted, and she heard the murmur of a male voice in the background, followed by Kel saying flippantly, 'I'm just making a date with the foxy lady herself... No, Mom's fine. Took herself off to bed when I got back... See you... Sorry about that, Challis.'

'Richard?' she guessed drily, and she knew exactly what he'd be thinking on hearing Kel's claim to be making a date with her.

'Just stopping off on his way back from somewhere. He is *not* thrilled about my new career, or rather my mother isn't, and he's worried about her.'

She wished he hadn't added that. It softened her resentment again, remembering how much he cared about his sister.

Later Challis shared a few of her thoughts with Zora, although she took care not to divulge anything she felt Richard might resent strangers knowing— thereby still considering the man, she castigated herself disgustedly.

'You see, apparently Kel's mother is seriously unhappy about his going into radio, and he's probably trying to set her mind at rest by introducing her to his colleagues.'

The things Richard had told her about his sister's life with a radio man had troubled her, and she hoped she would have a chance to meet her and perhaps ease her anxiety.

With that ambition in the front of her mind, she dressed as simply as she could for Saturday night's party, in one of the modest, scoop-necked shift-style dresses that were her personal choice when she didn't have to be in her Sounds FM persona. A deep, clear red, and only slightly clinging, she wore it with strappy sandals and her plainest earrings. Then, instead of her usual contribution of bite-sized goodies, she bought an old-fashioned apple tart, rich with cinnamon and cloves and criss-crossed with pastry, to take with her.

Dovale security was less ostentatious than the Keverne brand, but Challis had an idea it was the more efficient for being so discreet. After identifying herself, and being waved through the outer gates, she had to drive through nothing less than a mini-forest. Eventually a curve in the road brought her sweeping round in front of a mansion, airily graceful in the fading evening light, a pale grey-white building set in sprawling parkland dotted with great shade trees.

It all reinforced her awareness of the differences between her and Richard as she recalled the various modest homes in which she had grown up and thought of her present flat, comfortable and quite luxurious but still only a flat, a balcony overlooking one of Rosebank's busy streets as near as she came to having a garden.

Some distance away was another pale building, and she recognised her various colleagues' cars parked outside it. But if that was a cottage then what most people thought of as cottages were mere shacks!

Kel's half was decorated in black and gold. He gave

her a quick tour, the others remaining on the semi-enclosed patio, digging into the food and arguing about what music to play.

'Where's your mother?' she asked him just before he led her back to the patio.

'Her side.' He sighed with a mixture of tolerance and exasperation. 'She's still feeling a bit emotional about things, but she's not in quite such a state any more, and she seemed to like the idea of your all agreeing to come over here.'

'And Uncle Richard?' she enquired casually.

Kel hitched his shoulders upward and let them fall. 'Dunno. Out somewhere. But he said he'd come back later and keep Mom company for a while. He'll probably bring Julia—Julia Keverne. He's seeing her again, and she and my mom like each other.'

'How ideal.' Hearing how bitchy she sounded, Challis blushed with shame, hardly recognising herself. 'Kel, I'd like to meet your mother. Richard has told me more about the problem she has with your coming into radio. Maybe I can help?'

Kel studied her doubtfully and shrugged again. 'OK, I'll take you round, but don't stay long. You're here to party, remember? What's going on between you and Richard? He doesn't usually talk about family matters. I wouldn't call him paranoid, but he is fanatical about not letting strangers get close enough to gain any sort of intimate knowledge. But maybe you're not a stranger to him?'

Challis kept her expression impassive. 'We've just talked a bit.'

He grinned suddenly. 'I have to say you seem to have got on to personal terms with Richard if he's been talking about my mom's troubles. And what about this urge of yours to help talk her round or whatever? Isn't that beyond the call of professional duty?'

Four years older than him, she could get away with declining to answer, merely flashing him a laughingly quelling glance, but as he took her round to his mother's side of the misnamed 'cottage' she was reflecting that her relationship with his uncle had definitely become very personal, and, while she felt sorry for Lucinda Sheridan, it was really for Richard's sake that she wanted to help ease the situation.

CHAPTER FIVE

'YOU'RE the girl my son has been talking about so much this last year or so, aren't you?' Lucinda Sheridan prompted with a sigh. 'I used to hope it was just you—the attraction, I mean—but it's really radio, I know.'

Challis had always made friends easily, and, while she hadn't been too optimistic where this woman was concerned, Lucinda had proved an easier proposition than her brother.

In the second half of her thirties, she would have been at the peak of her beauty but for the greyish pallor beneath her recently acquired tan and the savage shadows scored into the skin under her eyes. Her colouring was the same as Richard's and Kel's, but subdued somehow, whereas theirs impacted instantly, giving emphasis to their vibrancy and male vigour. It was connected to her air of general tiredness, Challis decided, because although her manner was tense and nervy, her eyes contradicted that. They were vague and dazed, almost as dull as if she were doped, save for the spark of unhappy frustration in their depths.

Kel had gone back to his other guests after introducing them in Lucinda's lounge, an elegant room that spoke of excellent if unexciting taste, all cool pastels. The personal mementoes with which Lucinda surrounded herself reminded Challis of her own mother. Photos of Kel, Richard and a number of other people, as well as a cat and dog, and an album of

Kel's childhood on the coffee table, which Challis had already been invited to page through, were eloquent of Lucinda's love of home and family and a need to surround herself with the familiar.

'We're a good station, you know,' Challis ventured eagerly, praying she was doing it right—because what if she made things worse for these people? 'Reputable. We're strongly anti-drugs, for instance, and we support loads of charities in various ways... Oh, we're full of good works!'

Lucinda smiled at the comical conclusion, but her hands fluttered agitatedly before falling to fiddle fretfully with the material of her lovely pastel-flowered dress.

'Oh, I know!' she burst out miserably. 'I know I have to accept Kel's choice. I do accept it, but it's been a struggle, especially as this has all come about when I'm not at my best. I keep having all these stupid fears, but I am beginning to overcome them... Well, overcome my nature, really. Just because I've always sought stability doesn't mean it's the right thing for those I love. I have to accept that Kel's needs, like his father's, are different. I've come to realise that I don't want Kel to sacrifice his ambitions, waste his talent, just to appease me. I'd be riddled with guilt if he did. I think that's quite a big step for me to have taken, don't you?'

'Oh, it is,' Challis agreed warmly, meaning it sincerely, her pity for Lucinda now shot through with admiration. 'Won't you tell your brother that? I've met Richard a few times and I know he's worried for your sake and wants me...us to change our minds about taking Kel on.'

The request was impulsive, or perhaps a response

to the fact that her gaze had once more returned to the photo of a carefree, laughing Richard on the bookshelf behind Lucinda. He ought to look like that all the time.

'Yes, I must,' Lucinda agreed readily. 'He hasn't mentioned meeting you. Was he trying to interfere? Richard has always worried about me; he tries to shelter me to make up for... You see, he couldn't protect me when he was a boy, after our parents died, and I ended up in a disastrous marriage. But he shouldn't have to do it now and I shouldn't need it... Am I making sense? I get so tense and distracted these days. I'm supposed to take these pills, but my doctor is away so I'm seeing his son and he's changed the prescription. He's said to be brilliant, but I hate these new things; they're not strong enough but then after a while they're too strong, if you see what I mean?'

'Your system probably hasn't adjusted to the new prescription yet,' Challis offered comfortingly.

'That must be it. I suppose I ought to take them.' Lucinda reached for a pretty little pillbox on the coffee table and shook out three tablets before standing up with a grimace. 'I can't swallow them without water, like some people. Go back to Kel's party, Challis, he'll be getting impatient. I'm glad to have met you and I will talk to Richard... Maybe I'll come out and say hello to the rest of you if you're still here when these things start working and I feel more in control of myself; they take so long, though.'

Hoping she had made a difference, Challis returned to Kel's side of the building and joined the party.

Lucinda still hadn't put in an appearance by the time they were ready to make a move to a club that had been democratically selected after some bickering between the devotees of different musical genres.

Challis drew Kel aside as the others went to their cars. 'Shouldn't you tell your mom we're going? Will she be all right?'

'Richard will be here soon, and she took her pills earlier, just before you guys arrived, so she should be fine,' he assured her easily. 'What's wrong?'

Challis had paled. 'But she was just about to take tablets when I left her! How often——?'

'Oh, no! How many?' he demanded urgently.

'Three.' Challis was already on her way round to Lucinda's half of the cottage.

'The same as she had earlier. And three's the maximum safe dose, the doctor said when she asked him about taking more than the prescribed two twice a day because they're so slow taking effect.' Kel was behind her. 'Once they do work, though, they're incredibly powerful. She gets like a zombie, totally out of it... The first lot must have started working and she forgot she'd had them. She's had six, then!'

'Where is she?' Challis demanded as he started swearing, and a few seconds later they found Lucinda sprawled on the bed in her bedroom, having obviously gone to lie down. 'Call her doctor, Kel, tell him what's happened, how she's breathing and looking, how many we think she took. He must tell us what to do and be the one to call an ambulance if he thinks she needs one. I'm sure they're quicker if it's a doctor summoning them—I'll see how she really is and what I can do for her. I've done a first-aid course.'

Miles Logan had sent most of Sounds FM's staff on the course after one of their older DJs had become the hero of the hour when a silly girl had proceeded to add smuggled-in vodka to the drugs she had taken prior to attending a stadium concert the previous summer.

The trouble was that prescribed drugs weren't quite what Challis had been taught to deal with. She did what she could and then handed over to the doctor, who was with them in less than ten minutes, and was of the opinion that hospitalisation was unnecessary.

'I don't know who you are, but I don't think Mrs Sheridan or her brother would want you in here, sensibly though you've acted,' he told her, not unkindly but obviously intent on protecting the family's privacy. 'She'll be fine and Kel can give me any help I may need.'

Relieved, Challis went outside and round to Kel's side of the building, to find that everyone else had left. She was glad about that, for if the story of Lucinda's mistake were to get out, the Press were likely to take an interest.

Richard!

Challis discovered that she had begun to shake, a reaction to the fright she had had. Richard had to be informed. He would have a phone with him but she didn't know the number. She would go and wait in Lucinda's lounge, and when Kel emerged she'd ask him for it or get him to call himself.

As she made the decision, however, she saw Richard's car cruise up and stop in front of the big house, which somehow seemed to float, pale and ghostly, in the near distance now that it was properly dark.

She went to meet him, curbing an impulse to run as she didn't want to alarm him. Richard! He was going to be so upset as it was.

He must have seen her making her way through the well-spaced trees interspersed here and there by lovely round lights on pillars. Casually dressed for once, he came towards her after emerging from the car. No one else had got out, so he hadn't brought Julia Keverne with him after all.

'Date over, or just beginning?' he asked sardonically as they met, but then he saw her face as she moved into a pool of soft white light, and she heard his sharply indrawn breath. 'Challis! What's wrong?'

'Richard, it's all right!' Voice scurrying with her urgency to reassure him, she reached out, laying her hand on his arm, feeling the muscles under his warm skin knotted with sudden tension. 'Lucinda took too many pills by mistake, but the doctor says she'll be fine; he doesn't even think she needs to go to hospital. He's dealing with it here. Kel's there too.'

'Lucinda!' The light was deceptive, but she knew he had gone white under his deep tan as he shook her hand off and began striding in the direction of the cottage. 'This is your doing, letting Kel invite you out and agreeing, coming here and upsetting her, reinforcing her fears. I should have forbidden it when he told me, but I imagined he'd be taking you out somewhere—'

'It was an accident!' Challis was half running to keep up with him. 'Richard, she didn't do it on purpose! Don't think that—'

'With you here, on the scene?' he snarled furiously.

'I know, I do feel responsible in lots of ways,' she agreed emotionally. 'But—'

'As you should. You caused this. Your presence made her do it.'

'No! She made a mistake,' she protested passionately, a tearing sensation in her breast as she understood his anguish. 'We only realised when I asked Kel about her as we were about to leave. He said she'd had some pills earlier but I'd seen her about to take some more when I visited her.'

'You were actually *with* her?' Richard's rage boiled over. 'I told you to stay away from her! What the hell did you say to her to make her do this? Oh, I can imagine the effect you had—the impression you made. All mouthy and thrilled with yourself because you've snared Kel.'

'Please, won't you listen to me?' she begged desperately. 'Not now, but after you've seen and heard for yourself that she's going to be all right?'

'What for? Because you think you can sucker me into believing in you again? I know what you are, how selfish and ambitious you are for yourself; I've listened to you already, heard you pretending you want Kel for your precious station when it's really for yourself, the station and Kel. You'll go ahead and take what you want without caring a damn about what it might do to other people!'

She grabbed at his arm again but he threw her off.

'Richard!' Challis burst into tears as they reached the cottage.

His anger was really fear for his sister. She understood that, unable to blame him. He had lost too much, lost his parents way too young, and those who remained of his family were probably all he trusted and cared about; protecting them was his paramount concern. The possibility of losing his sister, or even just the realisation that he might have done so, was doing this to him, making him act like this, because he would be feeling he had failed her again, as he believed he had done at thirteen.

Richard obviously thought she was crying out of pique. 'Get out of here, Challis, and don't let me see you here again. If I hear you've been anywhere near Kel, I'll ruin you and your radio station. He won't be coming to work for you.'

Then he strode into his sister's side of the cottage, leaving Challis to cry alone in the dark for a minute before forcing herself to calm down.

She would only make things worse if she hung around now, so she found her keys and drove away sadly, using her cellphone to call Zora and confirm that she and Kel wouldn't be going clubbing. She went home, still inclined to give way to tears whenever she thought of Richard's distress and the angry, condemnatory form it had taken. This had upset her more than anything else had ever done. Not even her parents' most lacerating rows had left her feeling this bad.

She called Kel's number after she had been home a short while.

'Yes?'

'Kel?'

'He's next door with his— Challis?' It was Richard who had answered, belatedly recognising her voice, which was still slightly husky as a result of crying.

Unprepared, she hesitated and stammered, 'I... I w-wanted to know how Lucinda—'

'Don't call this number again, please,' he requested curtly, and rang off.

He really hated her! Challis shuddered with horror. No one had ever hated her before.

She tried calling again as soon as she woke in the

morning, and was relieved when she got Kel, but he lowered his voice furtively when he realised who it was. Challis enquired after his mother.

'Everything's fine,' he told her hurriedly. 'Look, I've got to go, but listen... Thanks for everything, mate.'

That misleading *mate* told her that Richard was probably around and must have instructed Kel not to have any contact with her. Challis sighed, recalling the way he had vowed that Kel wouldn't be coming to work for Sounds FM. Kel had signed a contract, but that part of it wasn't her business to worry about. Kel, Miles, their owner consortium and the lawyers must deal with it.

She was due to attend a charity fun-run Sounds was sponsoring, but, mercifully, she only had to get there for the end of it so she could take her time about getting up and dressed before driving to the finishing line to present a handful of spot-prizes.

Miles was there, but she didn't mention Richard's threat concerning Kel, leaving as soon as she could and driving the considerable distance out to the Magaliesberg to visit her parents.

All day she kept supposing it was distress over yesterday's events which was making her feel so bad and feebly unable to be enthusiastic about anything, but by the time she got back to her flat that night she could tell that she was in for the same forty-eight-hour flu that had hit a colleague a few days ago. Hadn't he joked about his germs being in the studio microphones?

She dumped the flowers she had taken from her parents' garden in a jug of water, without bothering to arrange them, resisted the temptation to crawl straight into bed and had a warm bath before finally doing so. She kept waking up all night, parched with thirst but too achy and weak to get up and do anything about it.

Her longest sleep came after dawn, and then someone rang her doorbell—and rang, and rang. When she could no longer ignore it, she reached for her watch and succeeded in reading its face after a few seconds' squinting. It was eight o'clock on a Monday morning, for pity's sake! Getting out of bed, she had to grasp the scrolled bamboo headrest, standing there swaying before putting on the nearest garment to hand, as she had slept nude, which was one of last year's Sounds FM T-shirts. The bedroom's vertical blinds were closed, but even so the daylight behind them splintered her head and made her eyeballs ache.

'Stop it, stop it,' she whispered frantically as she made painful progress through the flat, body and limbs feeling as if she had taken part in yesterday's marathon without training for it. 'Go away! Please!'

And of course the ringing ceased as she reached the door. Challis put an eye to the peephole and was in time to see her visitor turning away.

Richard! Her mind flew to his sister.

The key clattered in the lock as she inserted it, turning it the wrong way first, before getting it right and opening the door. The effort had used up her tiny reserve of strength. She got a hand to the doorframe and rested, head sunk forward, hair flopped over her face.

'I'd just decided you couldn't have come home last night. A heavy night, obviously? Serle Orchard, then, as I know it wasn't Kel?' Richard had turned back, and as she lifted her head sharply, yelping quietly at a streak of pain, he turned pale with shock.

'Richard—Lucinda?' Challis croaked anxiously. 'Is she—'

'She's fine,' he stopped her swiftly. 'What the hell have you done to yourself?'

'I'm sick,' she complained dully, in the wake of a surge of relief, 'and I'm going back to bed.'

Uncaring that she ought to stay and lock him out again, she turned and began to retreat, before having to pause, this time using the wall for support.

'Wait!'

Richard delayed only to close the flat door, and now he was beside her. He picked her up and carried her into the bedroom. As she was so slender, and only slightly over average height, he did it quite easily, but with her mind suddenly drifting deliriously, Challis reflected that he could have carried an Amazon without strain. In his suit. She giggled, picturing it.

As he placed her on her tumbled bed, she noticed that her T-shirt was bunched up around her thighs, and saw him notice the same just before he retrieved the duvet from where it had half slipped to the floor.

'I'm glad about Lucinda,' she managed as he covered her with it.

'What's wrong with you?' he demanded abruptly, frowning as he stood looking down at her.

'Achy-dying-of-thirst.' She ran the description of her symptoms together, but as he stirred impatiently she added, more coherently, 'Summer flu. It's around at work. Can you get me something to drink before you go?'

He went to do so without a word, returning to the

bedroom with a glass, bottled water and a mini-carton of glucose drink.

'Yes, the glucose.' She tried to lift her head from the pillows, managing a phantom version of her piquant smile. 'That's lucky. It's good for invalids too. I took it off a table in the tent at the end... There was a marathon, see? I gave out the prizes.'

He gave her a faint smile as he inserted the straw. 'Typical, you free-loader.'

He helped her manoeuvre her head into a comfortable position for drinking.

'I'm still too hot,' she told him irritably, when she had finished drinking.

'On fire,' he agreed drily as her hair fell back over her forehead after he had felt it. 'Who's your doctor, Challis? Do you have his number?'

'Somewhere... I don't need him,' she added, mumbling now.

'Yes, you do, and I'm not calling the fool who changed Lucinda's prescription, so where do I find the number?' Richard was insistent.

'He doesn't make house calls.'

'He will.' Almost menacingly.

'Run its course,' she argued inarticulately, before giving in and telling him where she thought the number might be.

Drifting between snatches of sleep, she knew he had found it when she heard him make the call in her lounge, obviously using his own cellphone, following it with another, telling someone he would be late and to cancel something and reschedule something else.

Why was he here? Then she stopped caring and went to sleep until the doctor came.

'Told you,' she said, when Richard returned to the

bedroom after the doctor had diagnosed that summer's particular strain of flu and departed.

He grinned. 'Being sick hasn't stopped you being lippy, has it? Do you have a spare key to this flat? He's left a prescription and it'll be quicker if I go and get it made up rather than having a pharmacy send their messenger to fetch it. Do you want another drink? You stole two cartons of that stuff, you kleptomaniac.'

'Not theft. A perk! Yes, please.'

Bringing it for her, he made sure she was comfortable, found the spare key to the flat—she heard him swearing under his breath as he searched for it, because she hadn't been sure where it was—and went away. He was back less than fifteen minutes later, with a quantity of green and white capsules and more little cartons of the glucose drink, which he said he'd found at the chemist. He put a couple on the bedside table, after watching her swallow two capsules, and left her to fall asleep again.

She hadn't thanked him, Challis realised guiltily, on waking around one o'clock that afternoon. She got out of bed, legs still wobbly, and went to the bathroom before tottering weakly through to the lounge.

'Get back to bed.'

Jacket off and tie loosened, Richard was seated on her couch, busy with a small computer, while an open briefcase full of papers and his phone lay beside him.

'I thought you'd gone.'

'Back,' he repeated, looking at his watch. 'Time for more of those capsules.'

Because she still felt as if she were made of straw, although less achy now, Challis obeyed, and he followed her to see she took the capsules.

Instead of sliding down into bed again, she stayed resting against the pillows he had raised for her, regarding him curiously.

'You don't have to do this,' she told him, voice still not quite back to normal, soft and rough. 'I know taking care of your own family is your great mission in life, but you don't need to do it for me. I can look after myself.'

'Normally, I know you can,' he concurred easily.

'What about your work? You've been here for hours.'

'I'm the boss, remember? I can delegate.'

'The hands-on kind of boss; I had the impression you wouldn't trust anyone enough to do that.'

'*Normally* I don't,' he agreed matter-of-factly, and she found that sad for some reason. 'Do you feel like eating something? Tell me what you want. I'll have to go out for it as your fridge and cupboards are bare. Don't you ever eat, except for the perks you score? What were you going to have for breakfast today, for instance?'

'Brunch,' she corrected him, detecting an exasperated note. 'I usually go out for it or eat an apple.'

'How can you live like this?'

He cast a disparaging glance round the bedroom which, although clean, because the flat was serviced, was untidy. Clothes, shoes and boots were strewn all over the place, the dressing table was littered with bottles of nail polish, make-up and jewellery, while CDs and books were stacked precariously on one bedside table, the other occupied by her small bedroom sound system and her regular and cellphones.

'I just do.' Challis was dismissive, thinking that their relationship—if they had one—was rapidly returning to normal if he was now in a mood to deplore her lifestyle.

'I sure as hell couldn't,' he asserted distastefully.

'Even with your tie loose, I believe you,' she retorted mockingly, and saw his face tighten.

'What do you want me to get for you?' he asked impatiently.

'Um, toast and Marmite? And maybe some of that soup you make in a mug. Chicken noodle.' She still felt ill enough to fall back on the sort of thing her mother had fed her whenever she was unwell as a child. 'I have got a toaster.'

Before she had become a DJ able to afford to eat out regularly, she had virtually lived on wholewheat toast.

'I was about to ask. Anything else?'

'Maybe some honey for my voice and—are these capsules antibiotic? I ought to have some yoghurt, if they are, but perhaps only when I've finished the course. I'm not sure. I think I can give you enough cash to cover all that.'

'Forget it.' Richard laughed suddenly. 'Although I appreciate the offer. I was beginning to wonder if this aversion to food you've paid for had anything to do with a miserly streak.'

'Just to do with time—lack of.'

'And the fact that you can't cook.' He laughed again as she looked cross. 'Well, can you?'

'Not really—not without the instructions,' she admitted, before something important occurred to her. 'Richard—'

'I won't be long.' He cut her short. 'Stay there.'

She had meant to ask him why he had been calling

on her this morning, but he hadn't given her the chance.

Before he left the flat she heard him answer a call on his own phone. 'Julia... I know, but you can trust your own judgement, I promise you. Yes, you can, so go for it... Good luck. See you.'

He sounded so warm and supportive, and it gave Challis a funny, wistful feeling, wondering what it must be like to be Julia, with the right to depend on him and call when she needed advice.

Impatiently, she waited for his return, wondering if she should put something else on while he was out, as this T-shirt wasn't exactly glamorous, but finally deciding she didn't have the energy.

'What about you?' she asked, when he was back and giving her the toast and soup—on a pretty little tray, no less. She had forgotten she had it.

'I'll get something later. I'm going to have to leave you shortly as I've got a final meeting with a delegation from the European Union that can't be rescheduled, since they're leaving the country tonight. Do you want to ask someone else to come in and be with you? I'll—'

'Wait a minute,' Challis interrupted determinedly. 'You've been here since the crack of dawn, and I'm grateful for all you've done, but I still don't know what you were after in the first place!'

'May I?' His face suddenly oddly expressionless, Richard seated himself on the edge of her bed. 'What can I say, Challis? Other than that I'm sorry, and thank you. For Saturday night. I wouldn't listen to Kel. I thought he was twisting the facts to ease things for himself, and for you, since he's so involved with you, but by late yesterday afternoon my sister started feeling well enough to tell me what had happened, or what she remembered of it—how she'd realised what she'd done and thought she'd lie down and wait a few minutes to see how badly the double dose affected her. I now accept that you had nothing to do with it, and I also now believe what Kel has told me about how you helped her until the doctor arrived.'

'Oh, it's all right,' Challis assured him quickly, moved. 'You were upset. I understood that. I don't blame you... You didn't need to do this—come here. Kel would have given you my phone number.'

'It needed to be said in person, face to face.' He paused, regret still darkening the amber eyes. 'I came here last night too, but you still weren't home by the time I had to honour a previous engagement. Oh, I might have used the phone, only I kept remembering... You cried.'

He sounded so appalled that she had to smile.

'Not for myself, so don't worry about it any more.' She sipped her soup and, seeing how sombre he still looked, she added teasingly, 'Haven't you ever made a woman cry before?'

He actually considered it for a moment. 'Not that I'm aware of.'

'Yes, well, I guess the women in your life have all been dignified ladies like Jools Keverne.' She'd bet a few had cried privately, though. 'Richard, I'm glad your sister is better, and thank you for coming here, and all you've done today, only please—never ring my bell so early in the morning again! Sorry, I don't think I can manage any more of this.'

He put the tray on the bedside table for her, and after a moment he smiled in response to her attempt to lighten the atmosphere.

'You're a very generous person, Challis. Lucinda has told me how you came to see her and urged her to tell me the things she shared with you, the fact that she accepts that Kel has to go his own way and all the rest of it... Incidentally, she's so embarrassed by what happened afterwards that she's decided to replace pills with counselling rather than ever risk such humiliation again, which is a relief. I never liked her relying on drugs.' Pausing, he held her eyes, smiling very slightly again. 'But I know I overreacted on Saturday. I suppose the whole thing was just another example of my tendency to take things too seriously, especially when you happen to be involved.'

'Because you had to grow up too fast, didn't you, when you lost your parents so young? All that responsibility,' she excused him promptly. 'Dovale Diamonds, with all its history and affecting so many lives; it was a tough task for you... You've never lived an ordinary, carefree—or careless—life, have you? You don't know how.'

'And perhaps I envy you yours.' Richard spoke slowly, picking up her nearer hand from where it lay outside the duvet and looking down, apparently studying her pale, slim fingers. 'Life's fun for you, isn't it? Although I still don't think I could live quite as casually as you do... Listen, I really do have to go. I'll come back tonight and see how you are.'

'What time? Because I'm going to skip going in to Sounds this afternoon, so I'll need to be there by at least nine tonight to get ready for my show,' she calculated as he dropped her hand—mercifully, because the warm weakness invading her in response to his touch had been a powerful distraction.

'You're not going to work like this.'

'I have to,' she insisted wanly. 'It's the first show Kel will be handling—well, second, after Angelo Goliath's—and I'm not handing him over to one of the old weekend DJs who do sit-ins. He's mine, he belongs to me, he's going to be *my* star deejay when Angelo and Miles have left and I'm running the station... Oh! You have lifted your ban, haven't you?'

Richard's face had stiffened woodenly and his eyes glittered angrily. 'Yes, you impossible girl. All right, if he means so much to you—but you mustn't drive while you're on medication so I'll fetch you and take you to your studio, and then collect you after your show and bring you home again.'

'It'll be one o'clock by then. Kel can take me home; you'll have done enough.'

For a moment he looked ready to contest it, but then he stood up and turned for the door.

'I'll tell him,' he said tersely, and left.

CHAPTER SIX

'How are you really feeling now?'

Challis turned from locking the flat door and looked up at Richard. He really was a tall man, probably even more than six foot, she guessed. He was studying her intently, golden eyes probing as they roamed over her face. She knew she still had a fragile look this evening, and the clothes she had chosen to wear for comfort's sake—fairly long and loose, a crinkle-pleated skirt in a dark pewter colour below a long-sleeved black button-up vest and her favourite go-anywhere black jacket—somehow accentuated her air of delicacy.

'The show must go on,' she joked feebly.

She felt weak, and slightly headachy, but her recovery must be underway if she was well enough to experience this stab of lust in response to his nearness. The fact that he was wearing one of his inevitable suits and looking distinctly unfriendly didn't have any neutralising effect.

'Kel knows he has to bring you home,' he offered as they moved along to the building's lift, 'and isn't he pleased!'

Richard seemed distant this evening, yet edgy at the same time, and she wondered what was wrong.

Being in the lift with him intensified her sexual awareness. She really wanted this man, and it just wouldn't do. But knowing that, deliberately emphasising it to herself, wasn't helping. Her flesh, blood,

whatever—oh, simply her weak woman's body, she
decided ruefully—refused to be sensibly influenced.

To distract herself, she said, 'You took off so
abruptly this afternoon you didn't give me a chance
to thank you for all you did earlier.'

'Forget it.' Richard was dismissive, his attitude still
remote.

Challis hid her frustration behind a provocative little smile.

'I really liked having you looking after me, you
know, which is weird now I come to think about it.'

It was, because she wasn't usually very good at
consigning herself to someone else's care, due to her
natural independence and a preference for doing
things her own way.

'It would be weird if I hadn't, given the straits in
which I found you,' he retorted drily. 'But, with hind-
sight, I don't think it was a very good idea.'

Challis felt it as a cool rejection, and, at less than
her resilient best, she found it wounding.

'Oh, right, you've had enough of me, haven't you?'
she challenged, defensively converting hurt into anger, so much easier to deal with. 'I drive you mad in
all sorts of ways, I know…the way I live, talking too
much. Maybe you should just let me get a taxi to
work?'

'I said I'd drive you and I'll keep my word, but if
you're still less than a hundred per cent tomorrow
you'd better make other arrangements,' Richard suggested indifferently as the lift reached the ground floor
and the door slid open. 'Perhaps Serle Orchard will
oblige you again.'

'I'm not seeing him any more.'

'Am I expected to believe you prefer a boy like

Kel?' Richard enquired sceptically, and her resentment surged.

'Yes, why not?' she shot back perversely.

Since he never believed anything she said when she was telling the truth, why not give him its opposite and let him disbelieve that too? The rebelliously contrary thought was feverish, a product of her physical weakness, she decided a moment later, as was the way his lack of trust had her suddenly close to tears. Why let it trouble her? He wasn't worth bothering about.

Richard ignored the defiant claim, merely giving her an inimical look.

Oh, yes, he was definitely reacting to having spent too much time with her today. A closer acquaintance had obviously entrenched his dislike, and, what was more, it seemed to have turned him off her physically as well, unless that was a result of seeing what a mess she became when ill. She couldn't detect the slightest sign that he remained attracted to her. Did he know it hadn't changed for her? If he did, that could be the reason why he now seemed so intent on keeping her at a distance.

He didn't even make a token effort at further conversation once they were in his car. A chatterer by nature, Challis soon found the silence unendurable, despite her awareness that he was likely to be irritated by any attempt to end it.

'Is your sister up and about again?' she began.

'Yes,' he said, curtly discouraging.

'I've been thinking about what you told me about her marriage,' she confided impulsively, 'and it really does seem to have been another version of my parents' relationship.'

'But your parents are still together, aren't they?' he pointed out in a distinctly quelling tone.

'That's what's just so amazing—the fact that they've never split up.' She shook her head, struck as always by the strangeness of that.

'So maybe they love each other.'

It astonished her. She stared at him curiously.

'You sound more idealistic than me—for once. I thought you were a cynic.'

'Not more idealistic, just older. I do have some idea of what love is.'

'And I don't have a clue?'

'How would I know? I don't know you well enough to be sure of something like that.'

'And you don't want to know me either,' she snapped.

'Because I already know all I need to. So, yes, Challis, I intend to stay right away from you from now on,' he informed her bluntly. 'Today was more than enough. The thing bothers me too much.'

'What thing? I'm not with you.'

'The feeling between us,' he elaborated harshly. 'If you hadn't been so sick and out of it earlier today, I'd have had a very difficult time keeping my hands off you. All I could think of was how much I'd like to join you in that bed, if only you were well.'

As usual, such frank talk warmed her blood, and she needed to swallow before finding a flippant retort.

'I'd never have guessed, but, like you say, I was out of it. But even now... You must be a brilliant actor, Richard. I was sure today's proximity and my being such a wreck had either killed your attraction or cured it!'

'No, it's still here.' Richard paused, and then continued very deliberately, as if making a formal statement, 'Against my will, I am attracted to you. The fact that it's mutual doesn't make any difference. As I say, it bothers me. I suspect it's also against your will, but you're not so troubled by it. You think it's a joke, an interesting phenomenon, and you're dangerously over-confident of our ability to control it. You can laugh about it; I can't. That's one of the essential differences between us.'

But it was his habit of being so honest about what he was feeling that got to her. It made *her* attitude look dishonest, especially when he didn't know how deeply affected she was underneath her flippant manner, which was the only way she knew of coping with something she found profoundly disturbing, and the more so just because it was so untenable.

'It's not such a big joke for me either.' She tried for her own form of honesty, her voice husky and low as she allowed her mind to focus squarely on how much she wanted him. 'I...I feel it quite seriously too.'

'And do you ache like I do?' he responded in a sensually deep voice, taking his hand off the steering wheel to let it rest on her thigh.

The fabric of her skirt was as light as parachute material, and she felt the weight and warmth of his fingers as acutely as if her leg were uncovered.

She drew a quiet, shallow breath, teetering precariously on the edge of yielding to sheer sensation.

'You're not doing your bit,' she reproached him thickly, utterly incapable of achieving the light tone she sought. 'When the thing's so impossible...sex isn't enough.'

'When we're worlds apart in every other way,' he agreed, removing his hand.

'So we shouldn't touch each other.'

'Right,' Richard concurred heavily, following it with a sardonic laugh. 'Do you know the thing that bothers me most? The fact that there was no need for me to let my life get entangled with yours in the first place now my sister has decided to accept Kel's choice of career.'

'Can't you just look on it as an interesting inter-lude?' she demanded mockingly.

'That's exactly how I'll look *back* on it, once we're no longer seeing each other.'

'Wasn't there anything good about it?'

'Oh, I know you've enjoyed it, haven't you?' he taunted, almost accusingly.

'Some of the time,' she acknowledged sharply. 'I certainly don't regret having known you.'

'The central way in which I want to know you would be disastrous for both of us.' The well-lit street enabled her to see the savagely derisive smile he slanted her. 'So that's it. No more. We part tonight and don't see each other again.'

'Without my having any say in the matter!'

Now why had she said that, sounding so full of resentment? She agreed with him; it was what she wanted. So there was no reason for her to be feeling so upset suddenly.

'None,' Richard confirmed ruthlessly. 'The thing is impossible. You know it, so there's no point in de-bating it now.'

She knew he was right. Challis had no more to say, and the rest of the short drive to Sounds FM was completed in silence.

Not to see Richard again... She watched his hands working the steering wheel. Not to know those hands on her body...

'You can just drop me off at the door,' she suggested as they were waved into Sounds FM's small car park, empty of all but two cars; Angelo's and Kel's.

What's funny?' Richard asked in response to the breath of laughter that came sighing out of her.

'Nothing really. I'm just realising how dead right you are—about everything. We don't fit. Look at those two cars over there.'

'One's Kel's,' he inserted expressionlessly.

'Yes, they're young men's cars,' she emphasised. Not that Richard was exactly ancient, but no one she had ever been involved with had driven his kind of car, or even a less expensive version of it. 'Hey, I said you could just drop me off. There's no need to see me in, so you don't have to stay.'

'Perhaps not,' Richard allowed tautly, nevertheless bringing the car to a halt at the darkest edge of the little car park and switching off. 'But I find there's one thing I can't deny myself before we call it quits, or maybe I simply can't resist the temptation to show you that an older man does have something to offer you.'

Something she wanted very badly at that moment, Challis discovered, understanding him perfectly.

'You'll get my flu.' She tried to lighten the moment as he released his seat-belt and turned towards her.

'I'd rather have that than the insanity I'm currently suffering from,' he returned grimly, releasing her belt now. 'Flu might be a small price to pay.'

'For what? And what about the security man outside?' she added agitatedly as he reached for her.

'In his little office with his eyes fixed firmly on the gate, I should think. Not that he should matter. He dismissed the objection and laughed suddenly, a strangely reckless sound that made her shiver. 'I don't believe this! Challis Fox gone all cautious, all of a sudden.'

'I'm trying to protect you, as *you* seem to be throwing all caution to the winds,' she snapped, despite the fact that they were in each other's arms by now, faces so close that her lips brushed his skin as she continued tartly, 'What if the guard or someone else recognises you and passes it on? What a come-down for Dovale Diamonds! Its president making out with a lowly DJ in a parked car! Wouldn't you hate people knowing you'd sunk to that?'

'I'm a democrat; I favour social equality.'

The throwaway answer was dramatically at odds with the way he began kissing her a moment later. This was serious kissing, she reflected driftingly, while she could still reflect. His mouth was so hard and hot, scorching hers, and she was melting, winding her arms tightly about his neck as she strove to get closer still.

She wanted him with a fiercely burning depth of desire she had never known before, white-hot and frantically insistent. Shaken, shattered by the voluptuously grinding pressure of his mouth, she moaned and shuddered, her fingers weaving themselves into his hair.

It had begun with *his* kissing *her,* but she was an equal, passionate participant by now, her mouth as hungrily devouring as his, wantonly urging him on, demanding an even deeper exploration from his lips and tongue.

When it ended, she made a tiny sound of protest, but he was only freeing himself from her clinging arms in order to pull her back against him until she was half lying across him, cradled in the taut strength of his arms. Arching erotically, Challis looked up into the face above hers. He had parked in the darkest section of the car park, but some faint yellow light still reached them from somewhere, a discreet light, just enough for her to see him by. Deep brown shadows filled the hollows of his face, but his skin was turned to amber-gold, as she knew his eyes to be, when night and his sudden mood of sexual heedlessness weren't making deep, dark, glittering pools of them.

'Richard...'

She didn't know what she wanted to say, just his name, probably, because it was his and he was the man she wanted. She couldn't have continued anyway. His lips were moving along her jaw and over her throat now, trailing blazing heat across her incredibly sensitised skin, making her gasp in an agony of delight.

And his hands...ah, one still caressed her side as he supported her with his arm, but the other—the other was moving confidently up over the front of her body, between the gaping edges of her jacket, long fingers competently unbuttoning the black vest beneath it.

Knowing what he didn't, that the effort of dressing while feeling unwell had led her to go bra-less below it, Challis tensed in anticipation, craving his touch yet half afraid of it, as if the reality of the intimacy she

was imagining might suck her over some fatal preci-
pice, a fall from which there could be no recovery,
no return to sanity.

Hearing his sharply indrawn breath as he discovered the truth excited her unbearably. His hand stilled
just below the full, taut curves of her breasts, and for
timeless moments he simply looked at her, the gleam
and shadow of his eyes seeming to feast on the
proud, pale mounds which her desire-swollen nipples
crowned like dark jewels in this light.

Then his hand moved up over one breast, his touch
almost reverent for a moment, before his fingers began to stir against her, so sensually, so sensitively
caressing, that she felt as if she were melting all over
again, her ravening desire doubly molten.

'Oh, you really are something superb,' he praised
her in an uneven, slightly hoarse voice as one finger
stroked erotically across and round her throbbing nipple.

The sensation made her whimper ecstatically, a
fine, helpless thread of sound, the sound of her total
surrender to pleasure. As if in response to it, Richard
shuddered and gathered her to him convulsively. With
a quick, harsh groan, as if he couldn't help himself,
he took the exquisite hardness of her nipple into his
mouth. Head flung back over his arm, Challis went
wild with the aching rapture of it, trembling violently
with the force of her passion, feverishly offering more
of herself, pushing wantonly into his caressing mouth.

It lasted only a few seconds.

'No, I must stop.' Richard was raising his head and
letting her fall back, his breath snarling in his throat
as he added determinedly, 'I *can* stop.'

She didn't want him to, but she could already feel

his rigid resistance, like steel. She drew away from him and sat up, quickly rebuttoning her vest.

'Then aren't you lucky?' she observed with rare bitterness, doubting if she could have been the one to do so.

Richard swore quietly. 'I forgot how sick you've been all day, which just shows how dangerous this thing is, if it can drive something like that out of my mind. Are you all right?'

'I will be.' It sounded as if she were talking through a mouthful of sand. 'No, don't come in with me!'

'Don't you have any regard for your own safety? That famous optimism of yours frequently strikes me as recklessness, in all sorts of areas. You've mentioned stalkers,' he reminded her, and she couldn't be bothered to point out that she always had to walk into the building unescorted when she drove herself to work.

'I'd have thought you'd be more worried about the possibility that I might start stalking you,' she submitted ruefully, not sure if she was more angered or embarrassed by the exhibition she had just made of herself.

'Thank you—I think.'

She laughed faintly, feeling close to tears. 'Come on, you can hardly be in need of such compliments.'

Sexually, as in every other sphere, the man couldn't have any ego problems. He had to be aware of how good he was, especially when a woman who knew full well that there could never be anything between them had nevertheless just proved herself utterly incapable of resisting him.

'But it is a compliment,' he asserted, quite seriously, as they began to walk towards the building, adding more lightly, 'Maybe I should change my mind about not seeing you again. You make me young, doing things like kissing in parked cars.'

'And aren't you ashamed of yourself?' she mocked.

'No.'

Just that, but with something in his tone to make her realise delightedly, 'You've never done it before, have you?'

'I seem to have jumped over my teens.' Reluctantly. 'And now here I am, chronologically burdened by your reckoning.'

She had to laugh, albeit with a softening sensation invading her heart, as she understood that there was at least one area in which his ego was indigent.

'Oh, Richard!' She gestured expansively as they reached the reception area. 'What's thirty-two? It's only ten more years than me. I don't really think you're ancient, you know. When I go on about your maturity, what I'm really talking about is—well, your affluence, your position in established society; Dovale Diamonds and your responsibilities to the nation, and the power and the glory and the suits and all that. If I thought you were old, I wouldn't have wanted to kiss you... That night the storm took out the electricity at my place, I thought I had a mission to give you some fun... If I have—in the car just now—don't you think that's a good note to go out on?'

She had to get rid of him before she gave in to the temptation to beg him to take a chance on her.

'Another appropriate occasion for a handshake?' Richard suggested darkly.

She gave him a wide smile. She knew that all this would return to trouble her later, probably in the couple of hours she spent winding down between the end of her show and going to sleep, but why spoil it for him?

'Give me five!'

A little to her surprise, he did, although with theatrically exaggerated restraint and with a smile like one of his diamonds, hard and brilliant. But he didn't say a word. Even after dropping his hand, he simply turned and went outside.

'That's all folks,' Challis murmured facetiously, smiling ruefully at the discreetly watchful inside security guard and heading for the cloakroom.

This was the only thing that made sense, she told herself firmly. She didn't want a lover she had to fight with.

Jostled by the other three members of the band as they emerged from the private lounge the hotel had provided for the interview, Challis shrugged off the guitarist's arm yet again, and briefly enjoyed a fantasy in which she snatched the tequila bottle from his fist and cracked it over his head.

Another illusion shattered. A wry smile curved her mouth. Oh, she was used to such behavior, but this lot had been particularly bad.

First of all they had reneged on a promise to come into Sounds FM and do a studio interview, demanding instead that she come to this hotel, one of Johannesburg's newest and most luxurious, situated in the up-market north. Then, when she had got here, after battling her way through traffic chaos caused by the rain that had begun early on Tuesday morning and still hadn't ceased three days later, they had given her nothing but trouble. Luckily the hotel staff had been obliging about providing this lounge on the mezzanine when she had refused to do the interview in one of their suites, but that hadn't been the end of her difficulties.

Declining the guitarist's invitation to go up to his room with him, she wondered how much of their raucous braying and howling had been heard by the hotel's other guests, or if the room was soundproofed.

Enduring their crudely lascivious, meant-to-be-witty farewells, Challis noticed that the mezzanine was unusually crowded with men in tailored suits and a handful of smartly dressed women. The double doors of the banqueting room on the other side now stood open, so the high-powered lunch a friendly member of the hotel staff had told her the Ministry of Trade and Industry was hosting must be over.

'Some mission of moguls from places like Brunei, Malaysia and Singapore meeting a bunch of local hot-shots—the powerbrokers, captains of industry, what have you,' he had explained.

Hungrily, she wondered what the menu had been—this hotel employed South Africa's most famous trio of chefs—and if there was anything left.

As the band finally made a noisy dash for the lifts in response to a reminder about soundcheck, their lingering manager laid a damp hand on her arm. At the same moment she caught sight of Richard Dovale and stiffened, because he was coming her way, looking directly at her, and even from this distance she had no trouble interpreting the disgust angling his face so harshly.

'Don't mind them,' the manager excused his band ingratiatingly, sliding his hand further up her arm. 'They're young.'

'Oh, is that what you call it?' Challis returned pleasantly. 'Young, rather than yobbish?'

He laughed sycophantically. 'I know how you feel! What do you say to showing me round this town of yours? Have a few drinks or whatever you're into, get to know each other—'

'It's a city, and I wouldn't wish your presence on its people,' she interrupted sweetly, freeing her arm and smiling for all she was worth, acutely conscious of Richard's approach. 'You have your own tape? The interview will probably be on between eleven and twelve on Monday night. Goodbye.'

'Ah, now don't be like that,' he protested, still smiling fulsomely but with something meanly vindictive behind it now.

'Challis,' Richard greeted her coolly.

'Hi,' she returned briefly, still wearing her false smile as the manager gave Richard a thwarted look and obviously found him intimidating.

'Look, I'll be seeing you,' he told her hurriedly, with a slight shrug of defeat, and went after his boys.

'Who was that?' Richard enquired distastefully.

The annoyance she had been subduing all morning edged closer to an eruption. She knew exactly what he was thinking, standing there in his millionaire's suit and regarding her so disapprovingly.

'Just a slob of a band manager. I had an interview.'

He really was intimidating when he looked like this. He took a step towards her, catching her unawares, so that she took an involuntary one backward into the lounge she had just exited a minute ago.

His eyes more topaz than anything else today, he looked past her to the empty tequila bottles, the array of used glasses, two lying on their sides, and the bits and pieces of once elegant sandwiches which were everywhere except on the plates on which they had been served.

'Interview or orgy?' In conclusion he took note of an overturned chair and the several cushions consigned to the carpet, and returned his contemptuous attention to her.

'Interview.' she said firmly.

Richard's lips curved without amusement as his hostile gaze slid over her disparagingly, absorbing her elegantly neat little black skirt, worn with barely black stockings and high heels, and the plainness of her black round-necked top, then returning to the colourful earrings she had chosen to compensate for the simplicity of the outfit.

'Interview, then, though it didn't look like that to me.'

Challis gave him a slashing smile. 'I hope you're not deluding yourself that you rescued me? I can handle that sort of thing.'

'One way or another,' he suggested insultingly, and her dark blue eyes blazed.

'It was *work*,' she emphasised.

'Just work? Not the chronic flirting I once suspected you of?'

'Do you mean you no longer do so? I don't suppose it's anything I said, since you never believe a word I say, so it must be your own judgement. You'd trust that before you'd trust me, wouldn't you?'

He gave her the strangest look, resigned somehow, but almost resentful at the same time. 'We can't talk out here. Can you still use that lounge?'

'What's wrong?' she taunted furiously, seeing how confidently he waved away a hovering member of the

hotel staff before forcing her to retreat properly into
the debris-strewn lounge by the simple expedient of
taking another step directly towards her. 'Worried
about being seen with someone like me after all?
There are always Press hanging around because so
many celebrities stay here... Or is it your peers you're
concerned about? Jools Keverne's imposing daddy?
He'll have been at that lunch over there, if you were.'

Richard followed her in and closed the door.

'You can stop implying I'm the snob here.'
Despising her with his eyes. 'I took the trouble to
listen to your show this week. All that laying down
the law about only taking fax and E-mail messages.
What about those listeners who don't have access to
either?'

'You're right, it's not democratic, and I do take
phone messages sometimes, but there are occasions
when it's just not convenient,' she defended herself
shortly.

She was glad she hadn't known he was listening,
although, had she done so, would she have been self-
conscious or provocative? She didn't know, but either
way it would have been unprofessional to let personal
matters influence her.

'Really? Like when you announce a *four-play* in
that sexily suggestive voice?' Richard drawled. 'What
are you doing all that time you're off the air? The real
thing?'

'Have you seen the inside of our studio?' she said,
scornfully dismissive. 'I'm usually *doing* pizza and
coffee... That reminds me, was there anything left
over from your high-powered lunch? I only had time
to stop for a doughnut on the way here, and look what
the band have done to the sandwiches. Those they

didn't taste, they opened, or threw around before I could get at them. And I swear, Richard, I'm going to stop telling drummer jokes on air for at least a week, because theirs was the only one of the lot who was half-civilised and actually tried to answer my questions intelligently.'

Richard's lips were beginning to twitch as he stared at her. 'How is it that your chatter can be both so infuriating and so disarming at the same time? What about room-service, then, if you're hungry? I can't bear this any longer. Let's see if we can get a room here for the afternoon. I want you, Challis.'

CHAPTER SEVEN

WITH her anger forcefully restored, Challis placed her hands on her slim hips, carefully French-manicured nails gleaming delicately against the black of her skirt, her attitude wholly aggressive as she met Richard's eyes.

'Why? Because that's the sort of person you've decided I am after seeing me with that tacky crowd? Or was it listening to my show that did it?'

'Because, damn you, do you have any idea what a hard time I've had staying away from you since I last saw you on Monday night?' It was explosively accusing, making her pulses jump nervously in reaction. 'I swore I wouldn't weaken, but it's as if fate—in which I don't even believe—is mocking me, because it's only Friday now and here you are! I can't win! And I can't fight you any longer. What better way to spend a rainy Friday afternoon than in bed, exploring what's between us and, hopefully, laying it to rest?'

'Sorry again! I think I've mentioned it before. One-night stands, even in the afternoon, don't do a thing for me.'

'All right, what about a proper affair, then?'

'And crucify each other while we're having it! You'd try to change me, I wouldn't let you, plus which you'd never believe anything I told you, and we'd both end up miserable and frustrated. We'd only make each other unhappy.'

And suddenly it was vitally important that she

should never make Richard unhappy. She wanted him, maybe even loved him, too much.

Oh! Rage roiled in her. That was why she felt so angry with him today. The man had made her love him!

Not deliberately, of course. He would probably be offended or horrified if he knew—

'So why don't you try to change me instead?'

'I know you're joking.' But suddenly she wasn't sure.

'Not necessarily.' He sounded reluctant. 'We're worlds apart, almost irreconcilably so—'

'But what you really want is for me to turn my back on my world and enter yours and conform.' Challis couldn't hide her resentment.

'It hasn't occurred to you that maybe I'd like to sample yours?' Richard held her eyes, an angry challenge sparking from his. 'Sample what I missed out on at your age because I was too busy trying to earn the respect of the people at Dovale Diamonds. Don't you think I envy you all that I missed, the sheer fun and freedom from responsibility? How much free time have you got this weekend?'

Sample. The word had such a superficial, impermanent ring to it. So did 'affair', however *proper*. Affairs were usually temporary. But, oh, she was tempted, her stupid heart twisting emotionally on hearing him admit to having missed out.

'None,' she answered him shortly, gathering resistance into herself like a shield. 'I've got to go to Sounds now, to set up my show. Then I've got a meeting with some people from a music store to decide on the format for a competition they're sponsoring, and I have to put in an appearance at a club gig after my show. Then tomorrow morning I'm flying to Nelspruit as I have a contract to compere one in every six Saturday nights at a new live music venue there. I won't be back until Sunday.'

'Cancel something,' he advised her urgently.

How had he got so close to her? Her pulses quivered.

'No way.'

'You know you want to.'

Oh, she did, when he stared at her like this, with desire glowing so hotly in his eyes, turning them a warmly golden colour, and with his mouth so sensually curved.

'Of the two of us, you were the more opposed to us—doing anything about this,' she recollected wonderingly.

'I thought I'd try cold turkey.' He had placed his hands on her shoulders, long fingers curling caressingly over them. 'I know, I shouldn't have listened to your show. Do you know how sexy your voice is? When I'm with you, seeing you, you look so seductive anyway that the sight distracts from the sound, but when your voice is all there is...'

It trailed away as she lifted her face, lips parting in helpless invitation as her swaying body came into contact with his and resistance shattered.

'Richard.'

It sounded as if she were falling or fainting as a great surge of physical longing came rolling through her.

'God, Challis!' Richard exclaimed in a hard voice, as if he were hurting.

The beautiful dark head was bent to her and she sighed into his mouth as it covered hers. Strong arms encircled her convulsively, gathering her up close, and the tidal wave of desire engulfing her became inexorable.

Irresistible and overwhelming, it was a wildly churning force, turning her body pliant and receptive as she clung to him and making her moan beseechingly when he deprived her of the devastating, sanity-robbing rapture of his kiss.

'I haven't asked yet,' he murmured huskily, his lips bare millimetres away from hers. 'Are you completely over your flu? I didn't get it, incidentally.'

'Yet.'

She couldn't concentrate on contributing more. Desire had put a strange darkness in Richard's eyes, and she was intensely aware of his raging sexuality, even more vigorous and insistent than she had known it before.

Greedily, her soft mouth snatched at the harder male one so alluringly close to it. She was trembling, and Richard was actually shuddering, as lips and tongues now became engaged in a ritual dance, teasing and tasting, at play, but such serious play—because he was a serious man, and he seriously wanted her.

She loved him, but how could she ever make him happy?

'No!' The agonising knowledge that she probably couldn't gave her the strength to free her mouth and tear herself out of his arms.

'Well, not here and now, obviously,' Richard agreed jerkily, glancing round the room with renewed distaste.

'I have to go to work,' she muttered, her brilliant mouth working as she stared at him with desperate,

glazed eyes, their dark blue colour deepened almost
to black by the pain of her dilemma.

She *loved* him! Oh, didn't that merit some degree
of risk?

'So when, darling?' he was asking, rawly urgent
but utterly confident with it.

'Not—' Distractedly, she shook her head, trying to
rid her mind of the dangerous idea invading it. 'Richard, you were talking about wanting to sample my
world. If it really is my world, my life, and not just
me you want to sample, why don't you come to the
Nelspruit gig with me tomorrow? Meet me at the airport. I'm on the ten o'clock flight and you should get
a seat easily.'

The offer was made before she had found the common sense to think it through. Loving him had made
her susceptible—reckless. She *wanted* to take the risk.

'I've got business appointments most of tomorrow,'
he told her abruptly, his dark face tightening.

'On a Saturday?' Sheer disappointment made her
scathing. 'All right, so I'm working too, but my work
is more fun than work, really. Most people's isn't.
That's why the Saturday plane is usually half-empty,
because business people tend to travel during the
week and most other people drive, as it's only about
four hours by road.'

He didn't answer her immediately, and Challis discovered she was holding her breath as she realised
that he was actually reconsidering her invitation.

Finally, he said slowly, 'If I did agree to go, we
could travel in my jet. It's small enough to land there.'

She laughed a little sharply. 'How modest of you
to have only a small one.'

'Some of our mines are in pretty primitive areas,

with landing strips to match. It's one of the few ways to get there.'

'Unfortunately the insurance Sounds FM took out for me means I have to use the stipulated carrier. Anyway, you're supposed to be sampling my world, and that includes travelling economy—assuming any planes are taking off at all tomorrow, with all this rain. I've heard there's some flooding in Mpumalanga. Oh, I loathe this endless, English kind of rain. We had enough of it at the beginning of summer and now here it is to spoil the end. I like our big summer thunderstorms, like we had that night the lights went out— lots of furious noise and spectacular lightning, and then it's over.'

Richard's mouth tilted upward at the corners. 'You would.'

She waited to see what else he would say, but when he stayed silent she was forced to ask, 'Will you come?'

'I'll think about it,' he vouchsafed reluctantly.

'I know, you don't really think it's a fair idea, do you? And you're probably right. But you're the one who supposedly envies my life. I don't covet yours, but naturally later on I'd be ready to—not exactly embrace it, but share—sample—some aspects of it in return. Although you'd probably be too ashamed of me to want me to. But that's fair, isn't it?'

'How very generous of you, Challis,' Richard drawled inimically. 'But I have to pass your test first, don't I? So you'd better be worth it—if I decide to submit myself to the trial.'

She flinched, realising where reckless impulse had led her.

'Wait a minute! We need to understand each other

properly. I haven't promised anything, you know. I've told you I don't believe in one-night stands, and you've talked about a *proper* affair instead, but if we spend the whole weekend fighting because of the differences between us and your refusal to have faith in anything I say, then we're not having that either. I've spent most of my life as a witness to my parents' personality clashes, and I don't need that kind of relationship for myself.'

Especially if he only *wanted* her, and she wasn't stupid enough to think he would allow himself to love someone like her. At least her parents had the excuse of mutual love.

'You're asking a lot—too much.'

'Then I'm out of here,' she snapped, guessing he was being deliberately offensive—probably simply because he did want her and had been tempted.

She found him beside her as she descended from the mezzanine.

'Where are you parked?' he asked.

'Visitors' car park.' She paused as they reached the great ground floor concourse, looking at a central display heralding Easter, which was still a few weeks away. 'Can you believe the way people adhere to the spring symbols down here, where it's always late summer or autumn at Easter? It's so northern hemisphere—and it's especially incongruous in here, with that indigenous mural.'

'You don't have much tolerance for traditionalists, do you?'

She gave him a triumphant smile. 'I'm too young, too African... That reminds me, Richard. If you change your mind and decide to hit Nelspruit with me after all, don't wear a suit—and bring something else for tomorrow night's bash.'

She was ashamed of herself as soon as it was out, aware that it was disappointment making her so malicious. To her surprise, Richard displayed no anger, regarding her questioningly.

'A Madiba shirt?' he suggested interestedly.

'Acceptable anywhere,' she confirmed happily.

Her heart was knocking with excitement. Was he going to change his mind?

He wouldn't come.

Challis watched the passengers for a flight to Sun City lining up at the gate before sinking deeper into her chair, sticking out her legs and absently admiring her newest pair of black boots, which she was probably going to spoil the first time she wore them since a pewter sky was still shedding rain outside.

She was expecting too much. Richard hadn't really given her any reason to believe he would change his mind yesterday. It had been wishful thinking on her part. Look at the way he had seen her to her car in absolute silence.

Of course he wouldn't come. The habit of being responsible was too well entrenched, formed too long ago, at the age of thirteen. The Dovale Diamond Company came first every time, or second only to his family, if he was even able to separate the two.

Another pair of boots appeared in her line of sight, facing hers, beautiful, fairly but not very well-worn masculine boots. Her subtly coloured lips stretched into a rueful smile. The wearer wouldn't live up to the boots. She never got that lucky.

Only this time she did.

'Do you have any idea how much I resent all this?' Richard dropped a black hold-all to the floor. 'Wanting you enough to fall in with your manipulative, mischievous plan?'

And his resentment was going to be another problem, Challis accepted, her heart thundering as she looked up at him.

'You're always so honest,' she observed almost reproachfully. 'You don't pretend, do you? I didn't think you'd really come after what you said yesterday. Dovale Diamonds can hardly suddenly cease to exist on Saturdays.'

'It's too big to collapse just because I take a couple of days off, as I realised when I thought about your invitation—or your challenge, and I think that's really what it was,' he retorted, dropping gracefully into the empty seat beside her. 'I can take time off. I can delegate if I want to.'

'I didn't imagine you'd trust anyone enough to be willing to delegate,' she confided impulsively.

'I can trust too—to a degree,' he added honestly, and suddenly gave her a blazing smile. 'I can do anything I want to, in fact.'

'A nice position to be in,' she mocked softly.

She knew it was true. This man could do whatever he wanted to, unlike most people. All that power and money set him apart.

'Especially if it enables me to take off for a weekend with a beautiful woman,' he agreed, idly humorous.

'Fun at last, fun at last,' she taunted, and sighed. 'You should grab more of it, because you're luckier than most people, you know. You can afford to have fun now, while you're still quite young… I was looking at the passengers for the Sun City flight, and they were nearly all elderly. I think it's because it's only at that stage that most people get out of the too little money, too many responsibilities cycle.'

'Or perhaps they sensibly preferred not to risk going by road, especially in these conditions,' Richard pointed out realistically. 'Thank you, Challis, but I am aware that I'm exceptionally privileged.'

'And I am aware that exceptional privilege comes with exceptional responsibilities,' she conceded fairly. 'I like your clothes.'

He gave her outfit a swiftly comprehensive look and laughed. 'I would imagine you do.'

Challis laughed too. He and she and probably half of Gauteng Province had donned a uniform appropriate to the weather: boots, jeans, T-shirts and leather jackets. The difference was that his had undoubtedly cost a lot more than hers.

Their flight was called twenty minutes late, and they took off in pouring rain from a decidedly wet runway. Once they were in the air, Richard left his allotted seat and came to sit beside Challis as the small plane, which had a twenty-nine-passenger capacity, was less than half-full.

'Where do you stay in Nelspruit?' he asked her.

'A nice hotel in town. You should get a room easily,' she added confidently.

'I hope to be sharing yours.'

He said it as calmly as if he fully expected to be doing so, and she slanted him a tart little smile.

'Don't you think it might still be a little too soon for that?'

'The sooner it's started, the sooner we can get it over with—and, yes, I'm remembering your stated rejection of one-night stands,' he assured her in response to her indignantly indrawn breath. 'But I don't imagine your expectations extend much beyond mine.'

Challis chose not to answer as the single flight attendant paused to offer them fruit juice at that moment. Richard was being deliberately provocative, probably to punish her for having dictated the game this far, but she also knew that she couldn't realistically expect an affair between them to last very long. Ultimately, the differences between their personalities and lifestyles would drive them apart in the absence of love's glue, since her love alone couldn't be enough, and he only desired her.

So why had she initiated this trip? She was only setting herself up for the worst kind of distress.

She looked through the window beside her. The clouds seemed thinner, an impression that was confirmed when a gap appeared and she was able to look down on a shimmering sheet of pinky-mauve and white on the eastern outskirts of Johannesburg.

'A great field of cosmos, but all drowned,' she told Richard brightly. 'Cosmos has always been the true sign of Easter for me, not all the spring flowers and baby chicks and rabbits people go in for... My mother grows flame cosmos in her garden, but I prefer the wild kind.'

He looked at her so curiously that she realised she could never have gone in for quite this sort of distinctly nervous chatter in his presence before.

'What's wrong?' he demanded directly.

'Nothing... Richard, what about Julia Keverne?' she added abruptly.

'What's our relationship, do you mean?' he

prompted, and smiled cruelly as she nodded. 'If this is conscience, isn't it a bit belated?'

Challis flushed angrily. 'Yes, it is, except that up until yesterday you had no intention of doing anything about what's between us, so I didn't need to worry. Yesterday afternoon I was...well, too distracted to think about her until much later, and then I decided you wouldn't even contemplate coming away with me if she had some valid claim on you.'

'Then I'm sorry for what I've just said, and thank you for your faith; it's a compliment,' he told her readily, the prompt apology startling her. 'And, yes, you're right. Julia and I have been close friends for years, but never anything more. We have a lot in common. She's had to deal with the users too, as Lucinda and I have, and whenever Julia has been sufficiently badly disappointed to go into wary mode for a while, she turns to me if she's in need of a partner for any-thing—if I happen to be outside a relationship at the time.'

'The users? Because of who you are?'

'What we're worth,' he corrected cynically. 'Haigh Sheridan was one who succeeded. Too many others have tried—with Julia, with my sister and with me. And more will undoubtedly target Kel in years to come. One woman already has, but we were able to disprove her claim that she was carrying his child. He has yet to go through most of it, training himself not to feel let down when the greed reveals itself, learning to question everyone's motives.'

'You thought *I* was targeting him, didn't you? Oh, I should have understood better why you were making all those assumptions about me,' she sighed regret-fully, following it with a reproachful look. 'In a way

I did, but you didn't really explain yourself properly. I would have made more effort to reassure you.'

'I hardly knew you, so I wasn't about to tell you personal things about the family.' Richard's lips twisted. 'We've occasionally let strangers get close before, when our guard has been down for one reason or another, and have inevitably had them try to take advantage of us. They're so damned devious about it too. If they were only honest about what they're hoping to gain, I'd have a lot more respect for them... But I don't need to worry about you, do I, Challis? You're only interested in me for my body!'

It hurt, although at least he now knew her well enough to trust that she wasn't materially motivated.

'If that,' she cautioned him.

He laughed softly. 'Emphatically that, and I've just been telling you what I think of deviousness.'

'All right! But I bet I'm not the only one, and you've let the users win if you believe I am. Masses of women must have been interested in you for yourself, and the same is going to be true for Kel. He's so like you, in his looks and his energy anyway. Our PA at Sounds is madly in love with him.'

'But you're not?' Richard was frowning.

'No and I'm not involved with him and never have been either.'

'Despite your acknowledged preference for young men?'

'Kel is just a bit too young... I suppose it's because of this other older woman who targeted him that you've been able to believe that I might be interested in him?'

A shrug. 'More specifically, because you're different—unconventional—and because the very first time we met you chose to give me a speech on the joys of toy boys. Mere mischief, I now know, and I have your word that you're not in love with Kel.'

He was accepting her word at last! But what if he asked if she was in love with him? Would she lie, joke or tell the truth, and how could she lie when it would justify all his past lack of faith in her word?

But he didn't ask. Challis relaxed, relieved not to be put in the unusual position of having to think before she spoke. Perhaps he thought in *love* was the same thing as in lust—if only where she was concerned. He had claimed to have an idea of what love was, and had credited her parents with loving each other—rightly, as she had grasped on reflection—so he must believe in the possibility of its existence. He just thought she was too shallow to feel it.

The flight to Nelspruit took only fifty minutes. The brief break in the clouds outside Johannesburg had been misleading. Mpumalanga Province lay hidden under a thick grey pall.

'We'll give it our best shot, folks,' the pilot promised, after warning the passengers that it might not be possible to land due to the fact that Nelspruit was suffering a drenching downpour and the limitations of the approach.

'You should return to your proper seat now, sir,' the flight attendant advised Richard, her eyes alight and lips curving in an essentially feminine response to his masculinity.

He gave her his most charming smile. 'Challis is nervous.'

She spared Challis an envious glance. 'Oh, well, I suppose it'll be all right, just this once. Are your seat-belts secured?'

'I've flown with her before and she knows I'm never nervous,' Challis protested crossly as she retreated.

'But have you ever flown in these conditions before?' he countered coolly, just as the plane bucked violently, dropping sharply and then rising jarringly, and she had to admit that she hadn't.

The pilot gave it several best shots, attempting the approach over the cloud-covered encircling hills a number of times, with much labouring sound from the plane's innards, until even Challis, who was truly a nerveless flier, found her imagination running wild.

'Sorry, folks.' The pilot finally admitted defeat. 'We've had a report that the cloud is significantly thinner and higher in the east, so we'll head for the landing strip at a private game reserve over that way. Nelspruit is sending joining passengers for Durban through by road and then the mini-buses will take those of you whose destination is Nelspruit back the same way.'

'I'm truly sorry about this, Richard.' Challis felt obliged to apologise.

'It's no one's fault,' he returned easily.

'I'd forgotten it wasn't a turn-around flight, that it goes on to Durban,' she admitted. 'I thought we'd end up returning to Johannesburg.'

As promised, the cloud became thinner as they headed east and the rain ceased. Presently, Challis could see the massively swollen Crocodile River beneath them, winding its way through sodden countryside very different from that around Nelspruit.

'What's wrong?' Richard asked quietly when she glanced at him uncertainly.

'That's the Crocodile down there. We keep on flying over it at the same place. There's a small hill down there I've seen three times. What game reserve did he mean? Is it even in South Africa, or Mozambique?'

Without a word, Richard undid his seat-belt and rose, strolling forward to the cockpit as coolly and confidently as if he owned the airline.

'No problem,' he reassured her when he returned a few minutes later. 'They're already in communication with someone on the ground at this place, and there's no need to worry about not having a passport as it's in South Africa. I know it well.'

'How long before we're there?'

He smiled slightly. 'Good question. They've never had to do this before, so they're not sure. They've got to find the place first, hence the business with the river a few minutes ago. They'd requested the safeguard of some visual pointers.'

Her dark blue eyes widened. 'Is there a reason to be scared?'

'None,' he promised her firmly. 'They're pros; they know what they're doing. And don't forget they're flying with enough fuel to get to Durban, as they wouldn't have refuelled at Nelspruit anyway.'

She sighed with relief. 'It's a bad omen for our weekend, though, all these problems.'

'A mere hiccup.' Somewhat surprisingly, he was much looser about it all than she was.

Eventually they landed in alien, sweepingly open pale golden countryside, dotted with marula trees which made Challis think instantly of elephants since they were said to get drunk on the fermented fallen fruit.

She'd worry about elephants later, she decided,

switching on her cellphone as soon as she was clear of the plane, amused to note half her fellow passengers doing the same, while the smokers headed for the shelter of a *lapa,* a thatch-roofed open-sided structure, cigarettes and lighters already out.

'I'm glad I didn't go into the cockpit and see how those guys were sweating,' she muttered to Richard, who also had his phone out as the pilot and co-pilot strode past, heading for the neat little office beside the landing strip. 'Where are we?'

He indicated the name across the front of the office. 'And it's an environmentally correct game reserve— no hunting, just viewing.'

'Yes, I've heard of it,' she agreed bitingly, remembering his claim to know it well. 'Visiting heads of state and other visible people come here, and the prices are out of this world, aren't they? Or out of my world anyway. You've been here before, haven't you?'

'As host to overseas business contacts,' he admitted, his tone hard in response to hers.

'I must phone,' she stated shortly, and moved away from him.

There was more bad news from her contact at the live music venue in Nelspruit.

'Listen, Challis, we're at the airport and they've just announced that this end of the road through to where you are is completely blocked. It goes partly through a gorge and the rains have loosened boulders the size of mini-buses. The people who were supposed to be joining the Durban leg of the flight are furious. You'll have to sit tight until it's cleared, and that won't be today. We or the airport will send someone for you as soon as it's safe. The customers will miss you tonight.'

'You've heard about the road?' Richard rejoined her. 'I'd hoped I could send for the Dovale jet to fetch us, but all flights in and out of all Gauteng airports are now cancelled as the weather there has worsened.'

'You couldn't have offered everyone a lift out anyway, so it wouldn't have been very democratic,' she snapped.

He sighed and spoke with exaggerated patience. 'When you've shrugged off that chip on your shoulder, would you care to consider our options? I've spoken to the pilots, and we can go on to Durban with them, as several people have chosen to do. It's fine there, so—a lascivious weekend in the tropical heat, Challis?'

'Can't, even if I wanted to,' she replied curtly, making it clear that she didn't.

'Your insurance again? Then we join the other passengers and returning Nelspruit residents, who all seem to be members of the regional government, and accept the reserve's hospitality. There are vehicles on the way from the lodge now, according to the pair in the office.'

'Can't afford it. Nor can Sounds FM.'

'Do you think the others can? They are offering us their hospitality, Challis.' An exasperated note now. 'I'll leave you to swallow your prejudices while I help those guys. Obviously they've never had to open the luggage hold themselves before.'

He indicated the two pilots, who were back at the plane and struggling.

'We only had carry-ons.'

'Not everyone travels so light,' Richard drawled,

'Do you always get this uptight and self-centred when
things go wrong? I suggest you think of others instead
of yourself. The older people, for instance, disappointed not to have been hugging their grandchildren
nearly an hour ago, and those two pilots, who did
something they've never had to do before and got us
here safely.'

He didn't give her a chance to respond. She
wouldn't have known what to say anyway. Bitterly
ashamed, she watched him stride away.

CHAPTER EIGHT

CHALLIS was ashamed of her behaviour. To make amends, she thanked the two gallant pilots and made friends with some elderly ladies, admiring the photos in their albums and being as optimistic as she could about the chances of getting to Nelspruit before the weekend was over.

The one thing she couldn't bring herself to do was tell Richard how sorry she was. It would look too desperate, too eager to please, and he might guess how much she loved him.

'What the hell is the matter with you?' He stepped on to her half of the elegant patio outside their beautiful double so-called lodge, finding her standing there disconsolately. 'I know you've only just got over flu, but you weren't this bad-tempered when you actually had it.'

'Well, how do you think I feel?' She vented her resentment stormily. 'Everything is happening to show me that I was wrong, and stupid, to suggest sharing this weekend.'

'Superstition.'

'No! Look at the way everything has turned out!' Her eyes were dark, flashing sapphires, and her mouth worked passionately. 'It's so ironic. You were supposed to be sampling my world, my lifestyle, and here we end up on your territory. This is your kind of place, part of your world, where I and these other passengers would never get to set foot but for an accident. I saw, I heard, how it was when you and the owners here met up; you were among your own kind. This is where people like you come to get away, and *"of course you'll have your usual lodge, Richard, it's been too long"*—and let me tell you I'd have demanded my own accommodation if it hadn't had this separate suite. That's why you were more relaxed than me after we couldn't land in Nelspruit; you knew we were coming to a place where you'd feel at home. But I don't! And here we sit in the lap of luxury while people's houses have been washed away. It said on the radio in the bedroom.'

'And I'm supposed to feel guilty about that? Although of course Sounds FM will rally round as usual, like they always do in a disaster,' he taunted. 'Sorry we're not so dramatic at Dovale Diamonds, but the housing projects we've initiated are all boring ongoing things, meant to reduce the number of people living in high-risk areas in the first place.'

'Oh, I know,' she granted irritably. 'I wasn't really getting at you. It's just that—I feel so humiliated! Embarrassed. It's all gone wrong!'

'Humiliated? In God's name, what for, darling?' His manner instantly altered by her tempestuous confession, Richard caught her hands in his, his lips quirking as he continued musingly, 'And who would have thought you could be so temperamental? It's the classic territory thing, isn't it? But I never dreamed you'd lose all that brazen self-confidence away from your own. In a way, I do understand how you feel, Challis, as on most of the previous occasions we've been in each other's company it has been on *your* territory, but there's nothing to be done about this right now. There'll be opportunities when we can reverse the situation, but in the meantime—why not enjoy all this, look on it as an unexpected treat? The older ladies are all downing cocktails in the main lodge and pocketing the swizzle-sticks and little umbrellas as souvenirs for their grandchildren. Get your jacket and come and view some game, at least.'

Challis gave him a sharp, angry smile as she pulled her hands away. 'You do it on purpose, don't you? You know I feel ungracious and ungrateful every time you mention those women.'

'Because you're too nice not to.' He gave her a quick, purely friendly hug. 'I know you, you see. Now, come on.'

What could she do? His eyes coaxed her with their glowing warmth, and he was being so tolerant and encouraging now that he understood the reason for her bad mood. If only he knew it, he was making her feel even more inadequate, all wrong somehow, and extra ashamed of herself.

She didn't really need her jacket, as it was so much warmer here than it had been in Johannesburg and her T-shirt was a long-sleeved one. Richard's was short-sleeved, and the sight of his dark, tautly muscled arms proved a constant distraction. They were such a beautiful rich bronze colour, and the fine covering of dark hairs was an emphatic, disturbing reminder of his masculinity.

He had caught her staring again, she realised at one stage during the drive they took in a Land Rover with a game-ranger. She lifted her gaze to his face and he raised his eyebrows in challenging enquiry.

Challis gave him a tart smile and lied, 'Nothing personal, just the respect due to anyone cool enough to do what you did. You know, putting on the jeans and the black T-shirt and not caring?'

It was rare in the trendy circles in which she moved, but Richard had the confidence to do it because he really didn't care, she understood. He wore suits to work because that was what men did in his world, and away from work he went for uncluttered comfort and probably never gave another thought to what he had on once he was dressed.

He obviously wasn't interested in getting into a conversation about his clothes as he didn't respond verbally, merely smiling slightly and watching her face. His eyes, such sexy eyes, were honey-coloured today, she decided, and what did that mean? Or was it just a trick of the light, created by the unaccustomed clouds in this usually sun-drenched region of the country?

Rare uncertainty plagued her, making her introspective. Was he really expecting them to become lovers this weekend? She didn't know what she should do if he was. She was aware that she was being irrational, but the way things had gone wrong today felt like a warning. She had been stupid to even consider the possibility of an affair with him, when she loved him and he merely wanted her.

The vulnerable beauty of a giraffe up ahead of them was a welcome distraction. In fact, Challis quickly found herself enjoying the novel experience of viewing game.

'City rose,' Richard teased in response to her excitement over even the ubiquitous impala and zebra herds. 'Or is that mall rat? Haven't you ever seen animals in their natural habitat before?'

'Only once, when I was very little. My mom somehow talked my dad into a conventional family holiday for once, and we went to the Kruger National Park for a few days, but I don't really remember much. Since then I've thought going to game reserves was superfluous, when there are so many wildlife documentaries on television, but being here for real is different somehow. It's special!'

And the fact that he was now being so charming, almost indulgent, made it even more special. Gradually relaxation added itself to her enjoyment, although one corner of her mind remained warily alert to any nuances in his conversation which might suggest that this was a prelude to seduction.

She didn't really think she had much to worry about, though. He wasn't the sort of man to jump on her and tear her clothes off if she made it clear that she didn't want him to.

The sun was setting by the time they got back to the lodge, which actually comprised the main lodge and a handful of free-standing smaller buildings. Each one was concealed from the others, the sprawling, exquisite garden in which they were situated securely fenced off from the wild outside, like an island in a sea that belonged to the animals.

They couldn't actually see the sun itself, just a brave slit of tangerine and apricot permitted by the layers of charcoal cloud along the horizon as it went down, obstinately romantic despite the killjoy weather.

Discreet little lights were already glowing at foot-level on either side of the path back to their own accommodation.

'Dinner at the main lodge?' Richard suggested, to her relief. She had already found out that those guests who preferred privacy could request service in their own lodges, and she didn't want that kind of intimacy.

Promising to knock at her door in time for them to have drinks prior to dining, Richard left her. Challis spent the time she was alone bathing and carefully painting her nails with the Rouge-Noir she had meant to wear for the Nelspruit gig. Her short dress was the same darkly dramatic colour, made of some chiffony material and utterly simple in style, held up by thin shoulder straps, and she had the sheer stockings and pretty pair of high-heeled shoes she had added to her bag of tricks at the last minute, in case she'd soaked her boots on such a day.

She had taken a peep into the central lodge's dining room earlier and seen that it would be softly lit at night, so she did careful make-up; softly gleaming lips and shadowy eyes. She hadn't brought any extra earrings with her, so the day's two little gold studs and single hoop would have to do.

She was in the lounge of her suite when Richard knocked. He was wearing a subtly coloured collarless Madiba shirt above discreetly fashionable trousers.

'Ready?' He appraised her outfit and she saw his expression change.

'I know!' she flared, abruptly as angry as she had been earlier in the day. 'It's not suitable for here but it's all I've got. It's my working uniform! I was expecting to be amusing the masses in Nelspruit, remember, not dining at an élitist place like this! Just be grateful it's not transparent and that I brought a pair of shoes with me.'

'Challis, stop it!' Richard took a swift step forward, lifting his hands to frame her face, forcing her to look into his eyes, urgent, angry and topaz at this moment.

'It's not like you to be so defensive, and you have no need to be.'

'I saw how you looked at me—'

'Because I couldn't stop myself thinking about what's under this elegant... What do you call it? Morsel?' he suggested quirkily, but with an underlying note of such raw sensuality that the heat of desire added itself to that of embarrassment.

'Then I'm overreacting, aren't I?' she acknowledged unhappily, trembling as his thumbs brushed along the hollows under her smooth cheeks, coming to rest at the corners of her mouth. 'But you're luckier than me. Madiba style goes anywhere. It's almost male national dress these days.'

'But you're younger and prettier and can get away with anything, so smile, my angel.' His thumbs lifted the corners of her mouth gently, trying to make her but drawing a laugh instead, and he was the one who smiled. 'And now you're going to have to put your jacket on, because it's cold outside. Leather and chiffon? I don't know.'

'Oh, no, it appeals to some people's proclivities, but I won't do that to you, Richard.' Trembling with regret—or relief—as he released her, she indicated the silky dark red shawl lying across a chair, a cobweb of a thing. 'At work, I'd be expected to wear it round my waist and have boots on my feet.'

He laughed at the defiant note. 'I can't wait to see it when we reschedule doing your territory.'

'Maybe.'

She wished. She wished there was some way they could have a bit of a future together. This afternoon on the drive, and even now, he had proved that he could have fun, could surrender himself to it, cut off from Dovale Diamonds and with nothing to be done about it. She was also touched, understanding what he was doing now—trying to reassure her, put her at ease with his suggestion that they would have time on her territory.

'Definitely.' He picked up the shawl and held it opened out for her to walk into. 'But for now, round your shoulders. It weighs nothing. Will you be warm enough?'

'It's not that cold.'

In fact, she felt too hot as he held on to the two upper corners of the gossamer triangle, pulling her in to him as if netting her before wrapping it round her and lowering his head to place a quick kiss between her eyebrows.

'Then let's go.' His smile was unexpectedly savage. 'Because if we don't go now, we won't.'

None of which exactly soothed her pulse rate.

At the main lodge, his status was reaffirmed. After a drink in the elegant bar with its African theme, their hosts, semi-celebrities in their own right, welcomed them at the entrance to the dining room and personally escorted them to their table, paying Challis the compliment of assuming that if she was with Richard she must be *one of them*—or had become one of them. Something someone said indicated that they were aware of her own peculiar celebrity status.

'All jolly old first names and gushing endearments,' she couldn't stop herself commenting when Richard had requested champagne, after first consulting her as to her preference, which was for *brut.* 'And your usual table, of course, Richard, *dahling!*'

'So, if "darling" is devalued, what are you going to call me?' he shot back, amused. 'You know,

Challis, I never dreamed you'd be so unsure of yourself on alien territory.'

'I'm not usually. It's just because—oh, I don't
know!'

The proud protest wound down into a pathetic lie.
Lying again. That was what love did, at least when it
was one-sided and you were driven to concealing it.
Because all this, the insecure feeling that she was on
shaky ground and her resultant moodiness, was because she loved this man. It wasn't that she was desperate to please him. She would never contemplate
remaking herself for a man, however much she loved
him. That would be a form of deception. No, he had
to accept her as she was, but on the other hand she
didn't want him to be ashamed of her. She needed
him to be confident that she could fit into his world
while remaining herself.

Richard was studying her thoughtfully, and it was
as if he had gauged the trend of her thoughts because
he said levelly, 'There was something you said at the
hotel in Johannesburg yesterday afternoon—that I'd
try to change you and you wouldn't let me. I don't
want to change you, Challis. I'm not arrogant enough
to think I could, and I'm sure you know that the reverse is also true. I can't change what I am for your
sake. That's why this thing between us can't last too
long.'

'So maybe we shouldn't let there be anything between us.'

His mouth tightened. 'There already is.'

Of course there was. She could feel it right now,
was aware of the sexual tension in him similar to that
which never quite released its hold on her whenever
she was with him. It was exacerbated now by the way

his golden gaze drifted over her, appreciative and possessive, so warmly wanting. She could literally feel it, outwardly and inwardly, her skin coming to life under it, her womanhood singing its siren song in insistent defiance of her mind's resistance.

In defiance of her heart's resistance too, which loved this man so deeply that it recognised its own vulnerability. If they became lovers, and then ceased to be lovers, she would never get over him.

'Yes, and I'm not sure I like it.' She tried for dismissive flippancy.

'You will,' he assured her, in a tone of such unbridled sensuality that unsleeping desire became a cauldron, a churning, boiling hunger for the erotic delights he was promising her with both voice and look.

'Here's our champagne,' she announced prosaically as it arrived.

Richard didn't refer to what lay between them so explicitly again, but she remained acutely aware that the matter was still unresolved all through the meal. She wanted him so badly, with an ache that couldn't be muted, and she knew he was feeling the same way. He scarcely took his eyes off her, his rich amber gaze intent on the expressions flitting across her face, or occasionally following the quick, graceful movements of her hands during the ritual of eating and drinking. The fairness of her skin dramatically accentuated the dark colour gleaming at the tips of her neat, slender fingers.

Nevertheless, their conversation was still personal at a certain level. He wanted to know more about her work and life, while his answers to her questions about his made her understand how little leisure time he ever had to himself.

Once she thought he was going to revert to their earlier tone when he said abruptly, 'Your hair always looks like one kind of flower or another.'

He was studying the way it curved in just under her jaw, satiny black, alive with blue lights.

Challis tried the quick smile with which she usually met other men's generally rather less imaginative compliments, but he had made her turn her attention to *his* hair now. It was so dark and smooth, lying swept back from his clever forehead, and she wondered what it would look like in the sleepy aftermath of passion, disarranged by ecstatic fingers—her fingers, of course.

Oh, God, the meal was nearly over and she still hadn't done anything to persuade him that they would be making a mistake if they became lovers tonight.

She deliberately took her time over her dessert, perfectly prepared crêpes of some kind liberally drenched in marula liqueur, and agreed to coffee afterwards, trying to neutralise her dilemma with common sense and failing. Why did she have to be so weak, still tempted despite the devastation she knew yielding would lead to?

Richard was quiet as they walked back to the luxury of their double lodge, and she couldn't rise to the bright chatter with which she usually filled silences either. She could feel his hand at the centre of her back, the lightest of guiding touches, and her nerves were screaming with heightened tension. She wanted to scream properly too, out loud into the enveloping blackness of a cool, cloudy night, because she had put herself in this position, rashly challenging him to join her on this trip.

She didn't want to be a tease, after all...

Sophist, she mocked herself. That wasn't the issue. She wanted him, but she couldn't have him because losing him would break her heart.

'It's still early,' he observed neutrally, when the door to her suite was open and she was stepping inside.

The interior's African decor was softly but warmly lit, and faintly fragrant with the talcum powder scent of a silent little electricity-powered mosquito deterrent.

'Richard—' Challis turned to face him warily and forgot what she wanted to say as he expelled a slight sigh, somewhere between exasperation and resignation.

'I'm getting the message, and in full, blazing neon, that you still need to do some talking,' he conceded flatly, following her in and closing the door on the night.

'Yes. Listen, Richard—oh!'

The door to her bedroom stood open and a light was on in there too, a member of staff having obviously been in to turn down the bed. The place offered many such old-fashioned services—but it was what lay on one pillow that had distracted her.

'What?' he demanded impatiently.

'Look!' Her natural *joie de vivre* reasserted itself. 'A chocolate on my pillow! Oh, this place really is to die for.'

He stared at her for a moment, and then laughed with real amusement.

'Free food—the acid test! There's nothing quite so guaranteed to restore your spirits, is there? I was half-expecting you to ask for a doggy-bag at dinner. Considering what food does for you emotionally, it's a miracle that you're so incredibly slim. But then you live at quite a pace, despite the decadent hour at which you get out of bed in the mornings.'

His gaze had gone to her figure, but it wasn't her slimness on which it lingered. It was her breasts, the proud fullness of which her slenderness so emphasised, and she could feel them tautening in reaction to his frankly sensual look. It reminded her of what she had, somehow, to say to him.

'Richard—' She broke off as he stepped round her and strode into the bedroom. 'What are you doing?'

'Come here,' he invited her, picking up the gold-wrapped disc from the pillow. But then he came back to her before she could either object or obey.

'You're stealing my chocolate,' she protested helplessly through shaky laughter, more disconcerted by this than by anything he had ever said or done.

'Feed it to me,' he commanded her in a deep, almost languid voice, unwrapping it swiftly and handing it to her. 'That was one of the most erotic things you've done, that time you tried to feed me at your flat. I wanted to eat whatever it was, and then I wanted to eat you. To taste every inch of you...'

And, help her, she was doing as he asked, lifting the flat round of chocolate to his lips because she wanted to, because she had to, and because he had made her fall a few thousand extra fathoms in love with him in just the last few seconds by proving himself to be so intriguingly unpredictable!

Instead of taking the whole chocolate from her fingers, he bit into it with healthy, even white teeth, his sexy lower lip just brushing her fingers, causing her to quiver. Then he took the remaining half from her and held it to her lips, smiling at her seductively after swallowing his portion.

'Richard…' Challis breathed faintly, and although her half-smile was tremulous her eyes were sparkling, because this was the man she wanted, the man who could do such unexpected things. 'You know what's said about chocolate… and honestly, I don't think I need an aphrodisiac.'

He laughed from deep in his throat. 'So have it just for the fun of it and because you like it. I'm not in any such need either.'

She let him place the chocolate between her lips, enjoying the sweet taste with some surprise because she had thought all the other sensations assailing her would distract her from something so frivolous. Instead, the flavour rush added to the pleasure of this whimsical exchange, and she caught hold of Richard's hand impulsively, keeping it close to her tingling lips as she savoured and swallowed the chocolate. Then she kissed his fingers one by one, her tongue darting naughtily over the smooth inner tips, rescuing a single trace of chocolate left on one before moving on to the hollow of his palm.

'Do you like that too?' he asked her huskily, his free hand carrying hers to his mouth.

She gasped, body and limbs turning to liquid as he drew one finger into his mouth and sucked gently. The next sound she made was almost a cry, certainly a tiny whimper, wrung from her by the sheer eroticism of his caressing tongue.

'Too much,' she protested with a despairing little moan, swaying helplessly until he released her finger, dropping her hand.

'We've done enough talking for now, haven't we?' he prompted urgently.

Now it was her lips against which his moved, and his hands were at her sides, moving up and down in an oddly restless rhythm as her shawl slipped from her shoulders to the floor.

Challis couldn't speak yet, lifting her arms to encircle his neck, with her hands caressing his head, fingers sliding into his hair.

Oh, she was going to suffer for this, but she didn't care any more, back to her reckless self again after the strange, fearful mood of the day.

'Kiss me properly,' was the answer she finally gave him, and he did, hard and hungrily, his whole body shuddering against hers as he gathered her in to him.

His mouth was so hot and demanding, plundering hers in a rapture of relief and anticipation, but she matched him perfectly, lips and tongue eager, almost frantic in exploring his, and she murmured protestingly when he eased the pressure.

'I've wanted you from the moment I saw you,' he muttered intensely, 'sitting there in that place in your ridiculous boots. I wished I wasn't coming to fight with you, that I could take you back to the bed you'd obviously left way too early and stay there with you. I thought I was losing my mind—hell, I was!'

'But you don't care any more?'

'No! No, I don't—I can't!'

'Nor do I,' she asserted passionately, kissing the dark abrasiveness of his jaw.

Richard was kissing her too, a flurry of urgent kisses scattered across her face, from one corner of her mouth over her cheek to her ear—her twice-pierced left ear as it turned out.

With a breath of laughter he raised his head, his eyes alight as he gave her a quick smile.

'You're not pierced anywhere else, are you?' His hand rested significantly over the region of her navel for a moment, and then moved lower.

'Find out,' she retorted wickedly.

His eyes blazed pure gold and he set about answering the challenge with quick competence.

She was unpierced elsewhere, and he found her beautiful. He kept telling her so, over and over, after the teasing and the laughter had ceased and they had yielded themselves to the sweet violence of their mutual passion.

Challis lay naked on her bed and Richard was shirtless as he bent over her, his mouth at her heavily aching breasts while she slid her hands over his smooth back, revelling in the feel of him, his strength and the sounds of pleasure that came from him. She couldn't be still, stirring restlessly against him in a rage of need, almost too sensitised by now to bear the sweet-sharp sensation his suckling mouth sent shooting all through her.

His fingers dipped between her thighs and her body clenched momentarily before surrendering to the exquisite stimulation of his touch. She murmured an inarticulate plea as his hand stroked down her inner thigh, and then up again, to where her body slowly seeped its soft, slippery betrayal of desire.

'Richard…oh, please hurry!' she beseeched agitatedly, almost nervously, as his sensitively searching fingers discovered her readiness.

Raising his head, he gave her a quick, hard smile of reassurance and withdrew to divest himself of the rest of his clothes. It took him mere seconds, but she waited in an agony of impatience, half afraid of some intrusion, physical, mental or emotional, that would make him change his mind.

Then he was turning back to her and she drew a shuddering breath, awed by his manhood.

Oh, she loved him. She loved the differences between them, his bronzed darkness in contrast to her fairness, and she loved his pleasure and lust, heard in the harshly appreciative sound that came from him in response to her touch, tentative at first and then gaining in confidence as she understood what she could do for him and, coincidentally, for herself.

When he lifted himself convulsively over her before swiftly coming down to her, her thighs gripped him like a vice. He felt so heavy, potently throbbing, pressing against her receptive moistness, and in another second that awesome, magnificent maleness entered her, deeper and deeper.

Challis called Richard's name in a tempest of rapture, giving herself up to the rare streaming sensation and hearing his choked affirmation of the same rapture as they convulsed together.

And it wasn't properly over. The violence of her ecstasy slowly softened to a made-of-honey feeling, and the long, vibrating sigh of complete sexual fulfilment passed between her lips.

'Challis...my sexy angel!' Richard exhaled the words on a similar sigh as he collapsed over her. 'So incredible, and that's just the beginning.'

Spent as she was, the words sent a thrill of anticipation coursing through her. They had a future...

Then the peace of bliss overtook her and she fell asleep.

CHAPTER NINE

SUNDAY was so blissful, spent mostly in each other's arms, that Challis half wished the road could stay closed for a week. But when Richard spent most of Monday morning on his phone, emphatically back in diamond tycoon mode, she remembered the classic old warning about being careful what you wished for lest it was granted to you.

Cut off from his world, and with only sex on his side to fill the emptiness, he would soon become frustrated, and their relationship wouldn't withstand that. It would be different if he loved her...

As it happened, the road to Nelspruit was declared safe that morning and they travelled back to Johannesburg the same afternoon.

Back in the city, their relationship continued, although it developed a pattern of its own, but at least they were able to observe one lovers' convention, as Richard was with her the Sunday after their return from Mpumalanga.

'Get up,' Challis instructed him happily, after they had woken and made love and slept briefly again. 'It's our one-week anniversary. Well, that was last night, but it's exactly a week since we woke up together for the first time, and I'm taking you out to breakfast to celebrate.'

Richard's eyes gleamed and he sounded touchingly intrigued as he confessed, 'The only breakfasts out I know are the power kind.'

'Well, this is for fun, and what's more it'll be neutral territory, because it's not one of my regular places. I read a review.'

She liked the easy way he fell in with the idea, and not long afterwards they were emerging from his car at the new restaurant, set beside one of Johannesburg's prettiest dams, both casually dressed in jeans but jacketless now that the recent rains were only a memory.

'Too late,' Challis laughed as her cellphone sounded. 'I was going to switch it off before we sat down... Yes?'

'Challis?' Serle Orchard's voice turned her smile to a scowl. 'Listen, there's been no action from that boss of yours about you-know-what, so I guess you must have toned the thing down—if you even really told him. I've been dense, I suppose, you clever girl. It was a tactic, wasn't it? One I should have recognised. Always reject an opening offer, hold out for more... OK I'll play. This new CD—'

'No!' Challis broke in violently. 'I'm not even going to argue with you about it, Serle. Just stay out of my life, never contact me again. I mean it.'

She cut him off, aware of Richard observing her impassively. He made no comment, and she was glad, but some of her pleasure in the morning had been marred.

It was only when they were seated out on the restaurant's sun-dappled patio and had ordered that he suddenly said, 'That call? Why is it still troubling you when you were so unequivocal? Second thoughts?'

'No! It's just...oh, the way Serle sees me, I suppose,' she confided, discovering it was a relief to do so. 'As corrupt, or corruptible. He was trying to bribe me, you see. Is that really the way I come across, Richard? You also used to have ideas of that sort about me.'

'But no longer, now I know you,' he assured her promptly, the warmth of his tone lifting her heart. 'As Orchard should know you. But it sounds as if he's too self-centred to bother with knowing other people properly, or perhaps he just judges them by his own standards. Forget him, Challis. He doesn't understand what you're about.'

'Which is what?' she prompted flirtatiously, his belief in her making her forget Serle.

'Fun. Flirting.' Now Richard's tone was complicated, likewise his gaze, but then he smiled. 'Definitely nothing sinister or inadmirable. Would you like me to add my voice to yours and make sure he knows to back off?'

'No, I can handle it,' she decided, since it was really a professional matter, for Miles to deal with if necessary.

The look Richard gave her held respect. 'Anyway, you were pretty emphatic, so he should have got the message.'

He was so supportive and understanding that her love suddenly felt too big for her heart to contain. She was so lucky!

'You are a lovely man! I know my insecurities are silly, but you take them seriously.'

'I take you seriously,' he returned rather wryly, and simply looked at her for several seconds before returning her smile so uninhibitedly that she was confident he now understood that he was the only man with whom she wanted to flirt.

The realities of their affair soon tempered that

Sunday's euphoria. It was the most reluctant affair she knew of. Each time they parted, they would stay away from each other for as long as they could hold out, before a build-up of need drove them back into each other's arms again. If she was the first to weaken, she would call Richard. If he was, he would simply arrive at her flat. Whichever one of them it was, the other would always be at almost the same fevered stage of desire, offering no resistance whatsoever.

Challis knew that was what Richard was doing, because she was doing exactly the same thing, although for a totally different reason. In her case, she was afraid of becoming too dependent on him, painfully aware that the more she had of him, the more she would miss him when he eventually took his passion away from her.

As for Richard, she thought he simply resented and disapproved of his own desire for someone so alien, and lived in the hope that it would cool sooner rather than later.

'Listen, I don't want to give you ideas,' she ventured truthfully, but keeping her tone lightly playful as they lay in bed early one morning after another erotic night of passion, 'but do you think this would…well, run its course more quickly, I suppose I mean…if we spent more time together?'

Richard had been smiling at her, but now he gave her a darkly considering look.

'I don't know, do you? At this stage I'm too involved to be analytical about any of this.' It was a typically honest answer. 'I'm like an addict, aren't I? I try not to give in to the craving, I try to sweat it out, but in the end…here I come again, looking for my fix.'

'And you resent it, don't you? But it's the same for me, and you know it. I'm just as often the first to crack.'

'The difference being that it doesn't really bother you. You just go with the flow. I envy you that ability, but you know my cardinal failing by now, my habit of taking things too seriously.'

Challis ran a hand over his chest, smiling with her eyes.

'But then a thrusting sex god is a serious entity in himself,' she offered with mock pomposity, afraid as always that if he gave too much thought to their relationship he would find that its inadequacies outweighed its pleasure and decide not to take it any further.

'Thrusting—' Richard's initial incredulity slipped into amusement. 'Is that another of your endearments?'

The business of endearments had become an ongoing joke between them after Challis had reintroduced the subject of his reference to 'darling' being devalued at dinner the night they had become lovers. It had grown into a competition in which they strove to outdo each other in outlandishness. Her favourite from Richard so far was when he had put on an exotic accent and called her his passion-flower.

Now she thought a moment, before smiling in denial. 'No, just a description, I think.'

'And somewhat over the top?' he suggested modestly, and she laughed.

'It's accurate.'

'Really, though, most endearments tend to be descriptive, don't they?' He caught her stroking hand in his and carried it to his mouth. 'Honey-fingers.'

'I guess you're right—lover-boy.' A shiver of unfailing sensation shook her in response to his erotically caressing lips and tongue.

There was a pause in his mouth's seductive play as he protested drily, 'Now that's definitely inaccurate.'

'There's not much boyish about you,' she conceded languidly, fingertips tracing the sensual outline of his lips. 'You're all man, and more adult than most. But then you were all grown up even when you were really a boy.'

'And you're so young still,' he commented, sounding almost reluctant. 'Not so much in age, but in your attitudes... Ah, this whole thing has such a *Beauty and the Beast* feel to it that I often wonder how the hell it ever came to anything at all.'

'Beast?' Challis was sincerely startled. 'Oh, you can't seriously think that, Richard! You must know what a beautiful man you are.'

Richard was smiling slightly. 'As long as you think so.'

'Anyone would!'

She lifted herself to move over him, kissing his mouth, her firm breasts pushing passionately against the hard warmth of his chest, erect nipples stabbing at him, and obscure shame burned in the back of her mind because she knew she was using sex to stop him thinking too much about their relationship and perhaps finally finding it expendable. Oh, this loving had her in a bad way if she could resort to such tricks, and yet there were many times when she sensed that Richard was also happier not to have to do too much thinking.

Later, when he had left her flushed and sated from his rampant passion, she continued to lie in bed, won-

dering which of them would hold out longest this
time.

He seemed to need her most often after he had
worked late, as if fatigue lowered his resistance. She
had given him the spare key to her flat and she had
twice found him waiting for her when she had come
home from doing her show. On another night he had
arrived even later, when the frustration of her endless,
aching desire for him had been hampering the usual
post-show unwinding process, so she had never really
come down off a high that night and their lovemaking
had been so intense that she had cried.

A contented smile curved Challis's slightly swollen
lips. However late Richard worked, and however tired
he might be, it did nothing to diminish his incredible
sexual vigour. She usually succeeded in saying something to make him laugh in the first few moments of
their seeing each other again, so perhaps it was that
temporary relaxation which replenished his energy,
because it was never very long before their opening
playfulness ceased and they gave themselves up to
serious pleasure which included *serious* endearments—or so she could convince herself when she felt
his throbbing, powerful presence moving in the slim
sheath of her body again and heard the passionate
names he called her mingling with her own inarticulately choked endearments. Then, she was granted the
beautiful illusion that he loved her.

Maybe tonight would be the one that broke the pattern, and Richard would come to her for a second
night in a row, she thought hopefully when she had
slept a while and woken, and was still lying in bed,
scanning that day's page of appointments in her diary.

Or should she call him and—well, sort of dare him

to make it two in succession? No, he'd guess how she really felt, and perhaps interpret it as a sign that she was becoming too demanding. Oh, she had to be so careful with this one-sided love.

It turned out to be just as well that she hadn't given in to temptation and perhaps won his agreement to come to her.

She was well into the third and final segment of her show that night when the studio line that was kept permanently open, its number known only to Sounds FM personnel and various emergency services, produced a call from Miles Logan. The DJ who was to take over from her at one had called him at home from the casualty department of a hospital to say he couldn't make it in tonight, having been involved in a mercifully minor accident on his way to work.

'The usual stand-in guy lives so far out, it'd be cutting it fine to get him in at this stage. I know it's very early days, but I reckon that with the skill he's already shown, our new boy can handle it, don't you?' Miles prompted swiftly. 'He's on top of the technical side, isn't he?'

'I'll sit in with him for a bit and see how it goes.'

Richard wouldn't be waiting for her as they had spent last night together, she assured herself, after telling Kel what had happened, impressed by the confident enthusiasm with which he'd welcomed the opportunity.

But perhaps she ought to call and make sure.

'Have we got a goodie for you! It's Kel Sheridan to take you through the night, and I'm here to tell you he looks as good as he sounds, girls,' she told her listeners in her most comically lascivious voice.

She pre-announced her play-out song, signed off in

her patent way and vacated her seat. The song was succeeded by the station's identification jingle, and another song to begin the next show, and then Kel introduced himself, as competently as if he'd been broadcasting for years.

'You've got me, Kel Sheridan and a whack of wicked music keeping you company till morning, and *I've* got the funky, foxy lady holding my hand, 'cos I'm the new kid on the block.'

As the next song started, Challis signalled with her cellphone, which station rules required to be kept switched off in the studio. Making sure he wasn't still on air, Kel spun round from the console.

'You're not deserting me?'

'Just stepping out to make a quick call in case anyone's waiting for me,' she explained.

'Red-hot new boyfriend, I suppose?' he guessed reproachfully.

'Sort of,' she admitted, understanding that Richard couldn't have mentioned their relationship and entirely unsurprised, because why would he?

'And there I was thinking I might grow on you, what with all the hours spent in close proximity.' He abandoned the woebegone manner. 'Look, if you've got something important on the boil, don't feel you have to hang around, Challis. I was born for this.'

'I can tell. But I'll stay a bit. I told Miles I would.'

She called her home phone number on exiting the studio, expecting only her own recorded message, so she was badly startled when Richard picked up the phone.

'You are there!' she exclaimed inanely. 'Richard, listen, I'm still at Sounds—'

'I've already heard,' he interrupted in a level but

biting tone. 'I always listen to your show if I can these days. That's how bad this thing has got. I know it's got to stop, and it's time to stop it, but I can't be the one to do it, damn you—'

'Well, don't expect me to be the one,' Challis flared, wounded, incensed, hating the resentment audible in his tone, unmistakable even over the phone.

'Are you doing it literally, Challis? Holding my nephew's hand?'

'No, I am not!' she snapped, and swallowed, weakening. 'This is a last-minute thing. It's his first time on air and I told Miles Logan I'd sit in with him for a while, but I'll be home as soon as I can... Will you wait for me?'

Pathetic woman, she chastised herself furiously. After the way he had just spoken to her—

'I'll wait,' Richard grated in confirmation. 'Drive carefully when you come.'

Then he rang off.

Disturbed, but seduced by the thought of him waiting for her in her flat, she didn't even remain a full hour with Kel, making him a last cup of coffee just before two and leaving him to it.

There was no shared laughter tonight. She found Richard lying in her bed, awake and with the light on. The sight of his bare chest and shoulders instantly, inevitably, ignited sexual excitement, because she knew he would be completely naked beneath the duvet covering the lower half of his body.

She was conscious that she should demand an explanation for his earlier attitude, but he looked so sexy lying there, summoning her with a smouldering, golden look, that all she could think of was making love with him. She couldn't help herself. She began undressing before she had even moved away from the door, leaving a trail of clothes strewn across the carpet: boots, denim jeans, rosebud-scattered top, socks and finally her satin underwear.

They made love almost in silence for once, the only sound that of their staccato breathing as desire mounted swiftly to an intolerably exquisite pitch. Then there was Richard's groan, harshly protesting, it seemed, as he entered her with a paradoxically ferocious tenderness.

'What was that all about?' Challis asked lethargically quite a while later. 'And earlier too, on the phone?'

'Jealousy,' Richard submitted succinctly, his typical candour even where his negative feelings were concerned something she loved in him.

'Because I had to work so late?'

'I very much doubt if you *had* to, but obviously you wanted to. No, I don't resent your work, Challis.' A pause. 'Jealousy of Kel, his freedom from all that prevents my seeing more of you, the absence of restricting responsibilities in his life, the fact that he shares your world and gets to spend at least three hours at a stretch in your company every weekday night.'

'In a computerised studio.'

Optimism rose. His jealousy had to be a hopeful sign.

'I know.' His faint laugh held self-mockery. 'I came here tonight—and it's the first time I've done so two nights in succession, which just shows us the way this thing is going, doesn't it? I came, thinking I might suggest that we turn this into a more regular kind of affair, eliminate all the empty nights—'

'Richard!' Her heart had lifted, rising so lightly it was as if it had been inflated, not with air but with the gorgeous, golden substance of happiness.

'But I wasn't thinking straight.' He punctured the miraculous bubble ruthlessly. 'I'm becoming too possessive already. Realising that while I was waiting for you tonight has helped me see clearly. It would be pointless to change the arrangement when it can't last too long, so let's keep things as they are, all right?'

'If that's what you want,' she conceded disappointedly.

'You don't sound as if it's what you want.' He turned his dark head, clever, suddenly alert eyes scanning her face, which she just had time to compose into a calmly smiling expression.

'I was just digesting it all… No, it is what I want, Richard,' she added very firmly, after the initial uncertain prevarication, because this was better than nothing, and if she demanded more he might take it all away.

Shame gnawed at her as she identified the malicious demon of dark thought capering spitefully in her head. Had she come home at her usual time he might not have got to this stage; he might have made the suggestion the extra time had allowed him to reconsider, and then she would have had him——because she would have held him to it.

'There hasn't been any change for you yet, then?' Richard prompted slowly, almost reluctantly.

'None,' she lied as blithely as she could.

He looked up at the ceiling again. 'It wouldn't have worked very well anyway. For instance, I'm flying out to one of our mines in the morning and I'm not sure when I'll be back. So I don't know when I'll be able to see you again.'

'Then sustain me for the famine to come by letting me feast now,' she demanded naughtily, once again afraid that he would start thinking too much.

She placed a hand on one of his tautly muscled thighs, her fingers seductively massaging as she kissed his shoulder. He laughed deep in his throat before gasping under the travelling caress of her fingers, and within seconds the conversation they had just had was forgotten in the throes of passion.

In the early morning he left her, once more deliciously languid, full and heavy in the aftermath of total sexual satisfaction. But Challis knew just how temporary that replete feeling was, and she spent her morning infuriating herself with futile wishing.

Miles Logan called her into his office when she arrived to make her preparations for her show that afternoon. They discussed station matters generally for a while, and then he said, 'Young Sheridan did well, going by the faxes we've received in response to the show. But I'm glad he's only been on the air once at this stage, as his voice won't be familiar, and especially not to breakfast slot listeners. Have you realised what the day after tomorrow is?'

'April Fool's.' She clicked, beginning to smile as she grasped what was in his mind. 'That thing we did last year was brilliant.'

'Yes, and as the breakfast format is so flexible, I want you and Kel to record something for it. His voice is unknown and you're good with accents... I've worked out a rough outline for you, but you'll need to develop a bit of a script—five minutes max. Let me have what you've done by this time tomorrow afternoon so we can make sure you haven't strayed into the actionable or offensive. There you go.'

She and Kel would fit it in somehow, Challis thought, giggling as she read through Miles's idea—a music industry news item which would purport to have come from one of their overseas sister stations. She couldn't get hold of Kel now because he would be at one of the outside courses Sounds trainees were required to attend, and she had a commercial voice-over to do, after which she must keep a promise to take a listen to the support band at a new club in Randburg.

It was only when she returned to do her show, having come straight from the club, that she was able to talk to Kel. First, though, she had to endure his comments about her outfit, the dress an ultra-feminine thing made from different kinds of white lace.

'You look like a bride,' he commented.

He was enthusiastic about Miles's idea, and they worked on developing it whenever they could during the next three hours, laughing most of the time and getting so carried away that they had to start again, censoring themselves severely when Challis decided Miles would definitely reject their first effort.

They had the script but nothing recorded by the time the proper replacement DJ for last night's accident victim arrived, wanting the studio to himself because he had someone coming in shortly.

'Now what?' Challis wondered frustratedly as she and Kel left the studio. 'The back-up studios are all sealed at this hour, since we had a bunch of equipment liberated one night, and Security don't have the authority to let anyone in. Miles wants to hear this thing tomorrow afternoon, and I've got a launch and a lunch before that, while you've got your course... The recorder I use for outside interviews is at home, but judging by that demo you sent us your recording gear is superior to mine. Can we use that?'

'Sure.' He looked gratified. 'Let's do it now, or is the new boyfriend waiting again? Oh, giving him the night off, are you? D'you want to leave your car here, or will you follow me home?'

'Follow you. You haven't got anything else on? A date?'

He shook his head smilingly. 'Only you... OK, Challis, I know. This is work.'

'Remember it. Then let's go—oh!' She hesitated. 'But I never saw any equipment at that party. It is yours, Kel? At your place? Not Richard's?'

She wasn't sure how Richard would react if she were to enter his house in his absence, especially as she had never yet been invited to do so when he was at home.

'Mine. I left out my studio when I showed you the place because some people seem to...sort of resent it, you know?' Kel gave her a curious look but didn't ask any questions.

Satisfied, she walked with him to the car park and got into her dark blue Opel Corsa, waiting for him to pull out first and following him to the Dovale estate, where he paused at the great outer gates to tell Security to let her through.

She glanced in the direction of Richard's mansion after parking in front of the so-called cottage. A few downstairs lights were on for security purposes, but it had such an empty air about it that she knew he couldn't have returned unexpectedly.

Unless he was waiting for her at her flat? No, he wouldn't make it a third night in a row, and she wasn't going to demean herself by calling to make sure.

'Spoilt brat,' she said when she saw the computerised sound system that Kel had in his own studio, including state-of-the-art recording equipment. 'Yes, some people might find it invidious. Poor little rich boy. Soundproof too, so we won't disturb your mom. How is she?'

'Fine. She's even looking for a townhouse, and Julia Keverne introduced her to some old cousin of hers who's asked her out. Boring guy, but she likes him. She's always asking about you. It's funny!' Kel laughed. 'For once she has the same idea as me, that you'd be the perfect girlfriend for me. Usually it's Richard who thinks more like me, and she's on the other side, but he was quite irritated when she started going on about it while he was here the other day. I don't think he approves of you, Challis.'

Challis actually blushed, well aware that it was more of himself in relation to her that Richard disapproved.

'Tough,' she said insouciantly, keeping her head bent, pretending to be examining his hi-tech mixing desk.

She felt as guilty as if she were actively lying, but if Richard hadn't told his sister and nephew about their relationship, how could she? But why hadn't he? Was he so ashamed of her?

It took her and Kel a while to record the ostensible mini-interview. First they kept corpsing each other, and then they thought of some improvements and had to do it yet again, but finally it was to their satisfaction.

'I'll take this and give it to Miles tomorrow afternoon,' Challis said, already on her way out.

'More coffee first?'

'No, thanks.' She took an appalled look at her watch. 'I must catch some sleep. I'll be good for nothing tomorrow as it is, and I've got to get up for this mid-morning launch.'

'You know, you really do look like a bride,' he observed, after seeing her to her car, plainly reluctant to let her go. 'So may I kiss the bride?'

It was such a boy's ploy that she laughed as she leaned back and put a hand on his shoulder to keep him firmly at arm's length when he would have come a step closer.

'For sure, when I'm someone's bride. *Ciao*, Kel.'

He sighed exaggeratedly and, still laughing, she got into her car and drove away.

She was just about to round the curve which would take her through the estate's mini-forest when a shadow detached itself from that of a tree at the edge of the road. She was driving slowly, so she was able to brake at her leisure when the shadow became Richard, his upraised right hand commanding her to stop.

'Richard! I didn't think you were home.' Her voice rang with gladness as she opened the window after engaging the handbrake. 'Get in and I'll turn round, or do you want to come back to Rosebank with—?'

'This is phenomenally—unbelievably—early in the morning for you to be up. What time is it? Just after three?' The silkily level voice couldn't mask the underlying fury, and if she had had a doubt left the anger vibrating in his ensuing laugh would have dispelled it. 'Another ten minutes and I'd have decided that you were at least still *you,* utterly unashamed of all you do! But sneaking out of Kel's place before daylight comes to give you away. Get out of that car, Challis!'

She was already doing it, instinctively putting it into neutral but not bothering to switch off either headlights or engine. Not because he ordered it, though. Anger, suppressed, even unrecognised, since their weekend in Mpumalanga, was surfacing. And not only surfacing; it was erupting, pouring from her in a lava-hot torrent as she understood what he believed.

'Unashamed? I am! You're the one who's ashamed, Richard, of—'

'Of myself, for being the fool I am—as I realised when I got home and saw your car parked outside Kel's place.' He had his jacket off, holding it bunched in a clenched fist, and his tie was loosened, giving him a dangerous, out-of-control air. 'You know, I was actually shocked, because despite all I've said to you on the subject in the past—despite all *you've* said—I never really believed that you could find a boy like Kel attractive enough to play around with. I didn't think you were quite that immature. I should have remembered that you're a flirt at heart who needs more than one man around, and now that Serle Orchard is out of your life… Which of my other early impressions of you should I have refused to relinquish? What were you doing? Staking a claim for the future while you thought I was safely out of the way? Because I'd said it was time to stop our affair? Because I'd decided against making our relationship more regular and reliable? So tell me what the attraction is in Kel's case. His body, or his connection with Dovale Diamonds? Do you think I'll part with a little hand-out more readily if it's he rather than me who's under threat from you?'

'Well, you would!' she flared shakily, confident of that much and close to tears because of it.

She bit savagely at the inside of her lower lip. She couldn't cry now!

'Oh, you're so right. I'm ashamed—'

'Of me, of me, of me—and of yourself for wanting me!' She was nearly shouting, shaking violently with the force of her long pent-up but finally released hurt. 'When you were talking about *Beauty and the Beast* I thought you were belittling yourself, but it was me! That's how stupid I am! You think I'm immature and inappropriate. That's why you haven't told your sister and Kel about us. That's why you have a key to my place and yet I don't have a key to your house so I can come round if I feel like it. Why is that, Richard? D'you think I might steal something? Why do I have to call you and virtually make an appointment? Oh, maybe I have got something to be ashamed of too, because—God, I don't know what's happened to my pride!'

Oh, yes, she did. Pride was one of the first things love stole from you.

'Oh, right! Present yourself as the poor, misunderstood martyr now.' Richard wasn't really hearing her, had given up to the fierce current of his own terrible rage. 'The trouble is I understand you only too well, lady. That's why I've so hated what I feel for you. It's diminished me. Well, you told me not to expect you to be the one to stop it, but you just have, Challis. It's over.'

'Oh yes, it's over,' she concurred bitterly, only just able to prevent herself stepping forward and attacking him with her fists. 'You've just proved a point I used to try to make repeatedly. We're too different; our separate worlds are too different. That's why you've reacted like this now, going ballistic—why you can't trust me! You automatically assume that my values, my morals, are different from yours—inferior, like me. Oh, we've got it two days early, Richard. The day after tomorrow is April Fool's Day, but here we are already.'

Her conclusion came through forced laughter, mixed with the tears she couldn't help, as she moved back to the car.

'Fools, yes. And the worst of it is the way I feel so betrayed—yet again!' The angry, accusing words came at her like hailstones, or bullets. 'Which makes me the bigger fool. I really thought that whatever the restrictions—or the limitations, rather—of the relationship for you, however ultimately frivolous and unimportant it was to you, you would still end one thing honestly before getting into another.'

'No, you didn't! You've never really trusted me. You don't know me any better than you did at our first meeting—'

'I thought I did, but what I knew to begin with was right! I should never have let myself be won over, ignoring what I knew. I wanted you to be special so I persuaded myself that you were—'

Challis was already in the car, jerkily putting it into first. She couldn't listen to him any longer, and she only just made it off his property before she had to pull over and give way to a storm of weeping.

CHAPTER TEN

RICHARD wasn't worth crying over.

Challis kept telling herself that, every time she felt her eyes filling with hot tears again. After the time they had spent together and the perfect communion of their physical relationship he still didn't know the first thing about her, or he would have understood that she could never have gone home with Kel for anything but the most innocent of reasons.

How could she love a man so lacking in understanding?

And a man who was so ashamed of what he felt for her, even if it was only lust?

Human enough to want Richard to know that he had wronged her, and to be feeling bad about it, she waited for Kel to say something to indicate that Richard had spoken to him and been apprised of the truth. But Kel didn't mention his uncle during the remainder of that week, or during the next.

Oh, why should she expect it? If he hadn't wanted his relations to know he was having an affair with her, he would be even less inclined to confide in them now, when it was over and he believed himself to have been a fool.

Even when he returned her flat key to her, with the correctness she would have expected of him, the day after they had parted, he didn't entrust it to Kel but had a courier service deliver it to the Sounds FM reception desk. Challis was just relieved that only Nicki

Adams, the receptionist, and an impassive security guard were her witnesses when she opened the little package that afternoon.

'An ex? Change your lock; he's probably had a copy made, girl,' the streetwise Nicki had warned her cynically, but she knew Richard had too much integrity to do a thing like that—and why would he want to?

The end of the following week brought the four-day Easter holiday. As a senior DJ she had a contract that entitled her to take both the Friday and Monday nights off, and she had already given notice of her intention to do so. The fact that she had done so in the wild hope that Richard might want to spend the entire weekend with her seemed to mock her now.

The four days loomed with such frightening emptiness that she called her father to say she had changed her mind about the invitation she had earlier declined and would join him at a jazz festival he was attending in Port Elizabeth. She caught up with him on Good Friday, after flying standby. Determined to have a healing, away-from-it-all break, she left her cellphone switched off and tried to give herself up to enjoying the festival. But even being out of Johannesburg couldn't ease the ache which occupied her entire being, cruelly refusing to be confined to just her stupid heart.

'Mom gave you a hard time about coming away this weekend, didn't she?' she ventured to her father when they met for brunch in their hotel's coffee shop on the Sunday, earning themselves the staff's disapproval when instead of ordering they sat eating the little praline Easter eggs from the pretty baskets her mother had insisted on sending with them.

'I gave her a hard time about staying behind with her house and garden,' he retorted, sounding tired but content, having been up playing sax and renewing old friendships all night.

'You're a strange pair.'

'It's love that's strange,' he contradicted her, 'but it works well enough for us.'

'Yes, my...my ex-boyfriend said you must love each other when I was wondering how you could fight so much and still stay together, and I realised he was right. I'm glad the both of you have got that.'

If only Richard could have loved and trusted her, all the other differences between them could have been overcome—and probably without the quarrelling her parents went in for, moreover, as they hadn't clashed properly at all during their brief time as lovers.

'Are you talking about what's-his-face? Serle, or something?'

'No, someone else.'

Her father grinned. 'I won't mention it to your mother, you butterfly. She's already making the time-she-settled-down speeches.'

'Then she's going to be disappointed,' Challis returned, far less blithely than she might have done not so long ago.

They returned to Johannesburg on the same flight late on the Monday and said goodbye at the airport as they had both left their cars parked there.

True darkness had descended by the time she reached her flat, and she could feel the teasing nibble of autumn in the air as she garaged her car, pocketing the keys and hurrying into the building's foyer by the back entrance which accessed the residents' garages.

She heard someone coming in through the street entrance as she got into the lift, but with less than her usual consideration she allowed the door to close and pressed the button for her floor. She didn't feel like casual company, agreeable or otherwise, so whoever it was would just have to wait.

Coming home at the end of a weekend was always a bit of a downer, similar to that Sunday-night feeling she had got as a small child, facing the hated prospect of school the next day until she had started enjoying it in her teens, but this was worse than anything she had ever experienced. She didn't want to be up there, all alone, without the hope of a visitor—or at least of the one visitor she craved.

Steps dragging and slow, she walked to her flat door and set down the carry-on bag which was all she had taken with her, extracting the soft little leather purse she wore suspended from a cord round her neck and hidden under her leather jacket. As she opened it she heard the lift come up again, and someone emerging, coming her way.

A true Johannesburger, she was automatically alert, wary but disinclined to panic, merely speeding up the process of extracting her flat key from her purse and ready to raise her voice in a homecoming greeting to a non-existent Arnold or Jean-Claude, should she feel seriously threatened, although she fully expected to see one of her neighbours behind her.

'Challis?'

Richard's voice was hoarse—with tiredness, she realised as she spun round, dropping the key, and saw his haggard face.

'What?'

It was a desperate, frantically defensive demand.

This wasn't fair! She wasn't prepared. She simply hadn't been expecting to see him again, and she didn't know how to handle it.

'May I come in?' he asked flatly, retrieving the key and handing it to her. 'You've had your cellphone off all weekend. I've been trying to find you, ever since I got back from the Netherlands on Friday, but Sounds FM and all the other bodies I asked naturally refused to divulge personal information. Your parents aren't in any phone directory, though I tried the few Fox numbers in the area you mentioned, and I couldn't ask Kel as he's been away somewhere for the weekend.'

'Not with me,' she assured him sharply as she unlocked the door and turned to face him warily again when he didn't respond. 'What do you want, Richard? The thing is over, we've agreed on that. Find someone else to help you satisfy your desires—'

'That is not why I'm here,' he cut in harshly, eyes glittering angrily in the soft light of the corridor. 'I need to talk to you.'

Still troubled by angry suspicion, she stared at him, noting the shadowy look around his eyes, amber out here, and the grimness of his mouth. As on the day they had flown to Mpumalanga, he was dressed similarly to her, in jeans, T-shirt and leather jacket, feet booted. He held something vaguely shiny in one hand, but the hot, turbulent emotions rioting in her heart and the questions rampaging in her head stopped her caring what it might be.

Finally she shrugged insolently, picked up her bag and opened the door, switching on the hallway light. Then she dropped the bag on the floor and stalked through to the lounge, without waiting to see if he followed her.

He joined her just as she had switched on that light and was shrugging out of her jacket, revealing the long-sleeved purple T-shirt she wore tucked into her tight jeans.

She gave him a brittle, taunting smile, noticing absently that he had both hands empty now.

'I can't think of a single thing I want to say to you, so you go ahead! Do what you say you need to. Talk. I don't promise to listen, though.'

'No, why should you?' He hadn't removed his jacket, but, like her, he remained on his feet, obviously as tense as she felt. 'But something you said—that night… It has been troubling the hell out of me. I was never ashamed of you, Challis. The reason I never asked you to come home with me but kept on coming to you here was because you'd seemed so disturbed and resentful finding yourself on what you thought was my kind of territory when we had to divert in Mpumalanga. I thought it would be easier for you if we spent some time exclusively on yours, until we were surer of each other and more at ease with the relationship.

'I also kept intending to suggest your taking me to some of these clubs you work at, but every time I saw you I just wanted you so badly; it got in the way and I couldn't think about anything else. But I have to be honest. The night I was tempted to suggest we make our affair more regular, more reliable, I meant to urge you to move in with me at home. I repeat—I was never ashamed of you, and if it had lasted longer there would have been functions in my world I'd have been proud to have you attend with me, and people I'd have been proud to introduce you to. Please believe that.'

Against her will, Challis was moved. It didn't change anything, but it was typical of the man to want her to know that, and it had been considerate of him to come and tell her—

Then her eyes blazed. How could she be such a sucker?

'You were too ashamed to tell your sister and Kel about us,' she snapped, and was startled to see a spasm of pain pass over his face.

'That was another kind of pride—the wrong kind,' he told her in a low, almost despairing tone. 'It was all just fun for you, most of the time, but it was so important to me. I took it so seriously, but I knew it couldn't last, and I didn't think I could bear their questions, my sister's sympathy and perhaps Kel's amusement, when it was over. So I said nothing to them and, God help me, I still haven't been able to mention you to Kel, so I still don't know what you were doing with him that night. I only know... You see, I've kept recalling how hastily I judged you when Lucinda took those pills, and I think I've done the same again. I don't think you are guilty of what I accused you of. I pray you aren't—damn it, I *know* you aren't!'

Challis swallowed as she heard his tempestuous conclusion. She loved a brave and honest man, and she knew how rare such emotional courage was, especially among his sex.

'Kel and I were working on recording an April Fool's joke for the breakfast slot,' she told him simply and quickly, although her voice shook slightly. 'I'm sorry, I should have told you that night but...well, I think I was too angry to defend myself.'

'I didn't deserve to be told,' Richard retorted, and shot her a darkly brooding look. 'Hell, to be honest, I probably wouldn't have listened.'

'You're always honest,' she observed between tears and laughter, beginning to feel awkward when he neither smiled nor spoke in response, and wondering where they went from here. 'Richard, what did you have in your hand when you arrived?'

He looked at her blankly for a moment before recalling, 'I left it in the hallway.'

He stepped out of the lounge for a few seconds and returned with a Cellophane box topped with a gauzy pink and mauve ribbon, holding it out to her.

'What—?'

'I had it done for you on Saturday because I wanted to have something to give you if I found you at home yesterday,' he confessed curtly.

'Richard, I...you— These are cosmos flowers!'

The box she had taken from him contained a plain chocolate Easter egg topped with exquisite sugar flowers, pink, mauve and white, unmistakably wild cosmos. Lips trembling, Challis raised her head to look at him questioningly.

'I remembered your spiel about northern hemisphere spring symbols for what is a universal festival, and what you said about cosmos being your personal favourite.' For the first time since he had appeared, he smiled, but only very slightly. 'You'll be happy to hear the confectioner thought that enchanting, and is thinking of starting a new line for next year. I drove out into the veld to get some of the real thing for you yesterday, but they've wilted since then.'

'Thank you. It's so gorgeous I want to keep it for ever, but I'm afraid I'll end up eating it.' Warm tears stood in her eyes.

'I wouldn't expect anything else.'

Emotion threatened to choke her, but then sudden, unexpected laughter rose. 'Richard...oh, you do know how to get to me, don't you?'

'It's not intended as a bribe, Challis,' he asserted shortly. 'I just...like pleasing you.'

'I know, and you do.' She waited a few seconds, but when he stayed silent, simply watching her, she was driven to ask the question which by this time stood burning in giant letters of fire in her heart and mind. 'Richard, are we...? Is our affair *on again?*'

'No, I don't think so, darling. I don't think I can stand it.' Her heart dropped shockingly as he lifted his hands, looked at them and let them fall. 'Unless... Challis, you don't usually let things trouble you, you sweep them out of the way, but I know this has upset you, that I've made you unhappy on occasion even if you've found it fun the rest of the time. So why did you bother to get into it? When we're so different? Do you love me?'

She blushed, hanging her head, but she owed him as much honesty as he had always given her where his feelings were concerned.

'Well, yes, actually I do,' she conceded grudgingly.

Then, as she lifted her head, she saw his face and understood what this meant to him. She let the Easter egg box fall on to a chair and walked slowly towards him—towards a man transfigured by joy and relief.

'I hope that's your only secret—lover?' she teased half angrily, and took him in her arms. 'You love me too, don't you?'

'Yes, Challis!' Richard's arms closed round her convulsively. 'More than life, more than the world... Since—oh, a long time ago. Consciously since that day I found you so sick. I wanted and wanted to tell you, but you kept going on about how different we were. I didn't think you could love me; I just started hoping you did, until finally I had to ask.'

'You went on about the differences quite a bit too, and how the thing wasn't going to last, or *I'd* have told you long ago,' she retorted tenderly.

'April Fools both of us, then.'

'Not any more, and never again either, as long as you understand... I know it has been part of the trouble for you, but while I may be a flirt, you're the only man I'll ever want to flirt with, Richard. I need you to understand that, because I can't do without you when there's so much else you do understand about me, like my odd little lapse of confidence when we were in Mpumalanga, and again when we went out to breakfast... I need a man serious enough to take me seriously, especially on such occasions.'

Then they were kissing each other in a rage of rapturous relief and fervent renewal, Richard's hands trembling violently as he ran them up and down all over her body, her own equally frantic on his.

Challis paused in the act of sliding his jacket from his shoulders and he turned her towards the bedroom. Mischief glimmered in her eyes.

'Can't I eat my pretty Easter egg first?'

'If you'll share it with me,' he shot back through a ragged laugh.

But they didn't get round to the egg until much, much later, when Challis slipped out of bed to fetch it from the lounge, returning to tell Richard about her weekend in Port Elizabeth and feed him pieces—of the chocolate only, because the sugar flowers were for her.

'The way to a woman's heart,' he sighed luxuriously, propped up on one elbow as he took his turn, placing a pink cosmos between her lips. 'Challis, you once mentioned the possibility of your being busy having babies some day in the future. Being a conventional man, I happen to think a wedding ought to precede the babies. Do you believe in marriage?'

'Only if it's to you.' Challis smiled demurely, and then spoilt the effect by biting his finger.

Pleasure flared in Richard's eyes. 'Then let's get married—in the cathedral, if they'll allow us. I want you, and everyone else, to know how proud I am to be loved by such an incredible, magical, good, bad, sexy angel of a woman.'

'There goes my credibility and your reputation,' she predicted, entirely happily, shivering deliciously as his fingers left her mouth to trail down over her body and circle the tidy little well of her navel. 'Hey! I could get it pierced if you like? My belly button. As a sort of wedding present to you?'

'Oh, I hope you won't, lovely!' He pretended dismay as his body copied the vibration of hers in response to her imitative fingers finding his navel's discreet hollow. 'Don't you know what these things are? The smallest, most intimate champagne receptacles there are, and nature's own design for nature's happiest drink on our happiest occasion. Since you've turned me on to your predilection for combining your favourite pleasures in life, I'd like us to toast our marriage that way.'

'How did I ever think you were conventional?'

Challis was smiling, voice bubbling and eyes sparkling. 'We could do it right now if there's some champagne in my fridge. I can't remember.'

'Oh, no, that's for after our wedding. Anticipation is half the enjoyment, so let's keep ourselves in suspense.'

'So we won't change our minds?' she guessed. '*I* won't, Richard.'

'I know. I've learned. I know I can trust you, Challis, because I know you wouldn't take the trouble if you didn't love me. I was teasing, but I think this Easter egg and you are enough for me for tonight, and you'll last.'

'For me too, as long as you last with me!'

In fact, neither Challis's credibility nor Richard's reputation suffered. Romantics and cynics alike were wholly intrigued by the match, and if the huge, glittering Dovale diamond Challis soon sported on her finger was the conventional real thing, its cut and setting were emphatically unique, and the dragonfly-inspired wedding dress she wore one morning in May was even more so, with its ritzy, figure-hugging bodice above a twirl of gauzy pleats.

She was a dazzling bride, her mother was thrilled with her son-in-law, her father's funky braces made up for his perfectly horrible bow-tie and were the envy of the Sounds FM male contingent, and Lucinda attended the wedding accompanied by her new friend.

Challis hardly noticed any of it. She only had eyes for the man she was marrying. Richard looked devastating in formal dress, and she couldn't wait to be alone with him and tear it all off him, and then they were going to do that thing with the champagne...

Kel got to kiss the bride when they arrived for their wedding reception, which was being held in Johannesburg's most fabulous hotel. He did so under the watchful eye of his uncle, who looked significantly at his watch after precisely one second and said, 'That's enough.'

He was going to be a possessive husband, Challis already knew that. Oddly enough, she liked the idea.

She met his eyes as Kel retreated and he took her hand, smiling at her.

'Party time,' she announced lyrically.

'After which, the real celebration,' he reminded her, voice significantly sensual, and then he laughed as he saw her eyes go to the bottles of champagne laid out for their guests in the long function room. 'And there's no need to go pilfering any of those, sweetheart. There'll be ample ready and waiting on ice.'

They wouldn't have far to go either. They were about to spend the afternoon in bed in a hotel room that Challis had once rejected, having booked one in this same hotel for the few hours they had at their disposal before flying to Paris that evening. Richard was going to be an indulgent husband as well as a possessive one; their honeymoon destination had been Challis's choice.

'You're happy, aren't you?' she prompted, still inclined to be awed by the knowledge that she had the power to make him so.

'If you are.' A serious man, he gave her the serious answer, but then he was smiling again and his golden eyes blazed with passionate feeling.

'Then you're happy, Richard,' she told him firmly, 'and that's all I want. Let's party.'

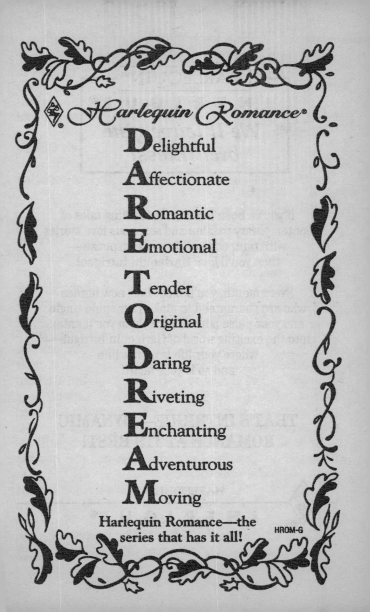

Harlequin Romance®

Delightful

Affectionate

Romantic

Emotional

Tender

Original

Daring

Riveting

Enchanting

Adventurous

Moving

Harlequin Romance—the
series that has it all!

HROM-G

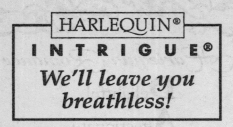

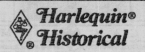

Harlequin® Historical

From rugged lawmen and
valiant knights to defiant heiresses
and spirited frontierswomen,
Harlequin Historicals will
capture your imagination with
their dramatic scope, passion
and adventure.

Harlequin Historicals...
they're too good to miss!